SHORT STORIES
Fantasy & Sci-Fi IV

Author's Website: www.richdisilvio.com

- - - - - - - - - - - - - - - - -

Names: DiSilvio, Rich
Title: Short Stories IV: Fantasy & Sci-Fi / Rich DiSilvio
Description: New York, USA: DV Books, an imprint of Digital Vista, inc.
Identifiers: ISBN 978-1-950052-00-4 (paperback) |
ISBN 978-1-950052-01-1 (eBook)
Subjects: Short Stories | Sci-Fi, Fantasy | Mysteries, Thrillers | Space | Vikings | Dystopian
Illustrations/Photos: 16

THE AUTHOR

Rich DiSilvio is a multi-award winning author of thrillers, mysteries, historical fiction, Sci-Fi/fantasy, YA/children's books and nonfiction. He has written books, historical articles and commentaries for magazines and online resources. His passion for history, art, music, and architecture has yielded contributions in each discipline in his professional careers.

DiSilvio's work in the entertainment industry includes projects for historical documentaries, including James Cameron's *The Lost Tomb of Jesus, Killing Hitler, The War Zone* series, *Return to Kirkuk, Operation Valkyrie*, and cable TV shows and films such as *Tracey Ullman's State of the Union, Celebrity Mole, Blood Ties, Monty Python: Almost the Truth*, and many others.

He has written commentaries on the great composers (such as the Franz Liszt Site), and conceived and designed the Pantheon of Composers porcelain collection for the Metropolitan Opera, which also retailed throughout the USA and Europe.

His artwork and new media projects have graced the album covers and animated advertisements for numerous super-groups and celebrities, including, Pink Floyd, Yes, The Moody Blues, Cher, Madonna, Jay-Z, Willie Nelson, Miles Davis, the Rolling Stones, Alice Cooper, Queen, and many more.

As a software designer/developer, Rich pioneered the first interactive CD-ROM for educating staff and parents about Applied Behavioral Analysis (ABA) for training individuals with autism.

Rich lives in New York with his wife and has four children.

Contents

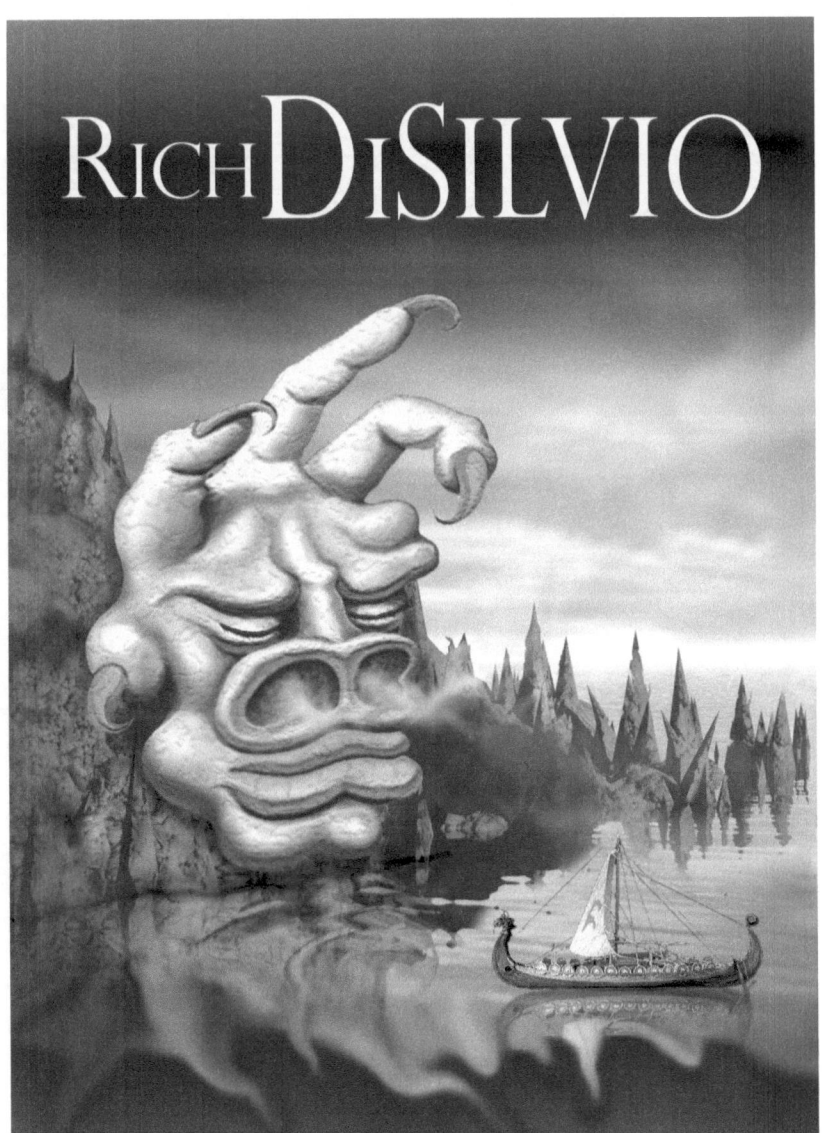

THE STONE BALLS OF ABERDEEN

John Halford sat at the bar in Tim's Tavern in Aberdeen, Scotland, gazing through his covetous, Scotch-soused eyes at the photo of Craigievar Castle in the daily newspaper. As he read the blurry lines of print, he seethed.

Meanwhile, the eighty-year-old owner/bartender wiped the bar-top clean with a beer-soaked rag and said in his thick brogue, "John, ol' boy. Why do ya torment yaself readin' about that damned castle? The state owns it now, so it ain't eva gonna be yars!"

John peered up at old Tim out of the corner of his eye. "But it damn well ought to be mine! You know the shenanigans that went on. The bloody buggers ripped it right out of my hands. It just ain't fair! And you know it."

"Ah, stop yar bellyaching. Let it go, John. It'll be the death of ya."

John ignored him, took another swig of his Chivas Regal, and peered back at the irritating advertisement by the

1

National Trust for Scotland, which heralded the castle's completion in 1626 and its pretty, pinkish harled finish—the stucco-like coating that molded its smooth exterior walls. Having been turned into a museum, the NTS offered special tours celebrating the castle's historical significance in Aberdeenshire.

John couldn't get out of his head the bizarre means by which he'd been gypped out of his inheritance. As he read the article, it once again ignited his furor about how his cousin, William Forbes, had once held the baronetcy and large estate, which included the majestic Craigievar Castle. William had died in 1965, and, according to tradition, the next male in line—John!—was to inherit the baronetcy. William's only sibling was Elizabeth, a transgender who had re-registered her birth thirteen years before William's death as a male, taking on the new name of Ewan and stealing John's regal inheritance. Further fueling John's animosity was that after a private court battle to win possession, Ewan had foolishly handed Craigievar Castle over to the National Trust for Scotland.

It was now 1999, and John had spent the better part of his sixty-eight-years on the planet pining for the castle that should have been his. That he was forced into a foster home at age nine—after his parents died during World War II, and his Forbes relatives disowned him—also stuck a needle in his side, one he could never seem to remove. But as John figured it, winning back his castle would soothe much of the misery and misfortune that plagued his long, meaningless life.

John gazed at the photo of *his* castle, then at the smaller photo of his deceased cousin, Ewan. His booze-glazed eyes glowed redder with anger as his mind raced. *There's nothing I can do about* you, *Ewan, you dead freak. But, one way or another, I'll get that castle out of Scotland's hands and into my rightful mitts!*

With that, John tossed the newspaper on to the bar, swallowed the last gulp of his Scotch, and staggered out the door. Oblivious to everyone and everything in the quaint township, John walked along the sidewalk the mere two blocks to his shabby apartment, while the nearby sounds of waves crashing on the seashore and the smell of salty air permeated the brisk Scottish atmosphere.

John tried several times to stick the key into the door lock with his shaky hand, but failed. He struggled to focus his lubricated eyes, but only grew more irritated. After hacking up the brass lock plate—which had been abused many times before in a similar fashion—John eventually found the keyhole and pushed his way into his flat. As he took a step, he slipped on the pile of unpaid invoices and summonses on the floor. He caught his balance, looked down, and snarled; they were the same damned irritants that prompted his trip to the pub in the first place.

He plopped on the couch and rubbed his throbbing head. *How the hell could someone with* my *noble blood be stuck in a shithole like* this?—*one I can't even afford!* He punched the arm of the frayed old couch. *This is bullshit!*

John gazed back at the pile of depressing envelopes on the floor, gritted his teeth, and marched out of the flat once again, refusing to sit and stare at reminders of his shitty lot in life.

He hopped in his beat-up '79 MG Midget and drove aimlessly out of the seaside village of Aberdeen and into the countrified streets of rural Scotland. Some forty-five minutes later, he ended up in Alford. Sullen, and with his mind in a rancid fog, John pulled over. He sat for a moment, gazing blindly into space, then unthinkingly opened the door and got out. He walked slowly along the roadside several meters, then veered onto a sprawling meadow. The beauty of the rolling hills and trees helped to soothe his woes, while the alcohol that numbed his brain slowly dissipated with each breath of fresh air.

As he shuffled through the tall grass, John suddenly tripped. Catching his balance, he spun around and scanned the terrain for the culprit. That's when his eyes landed on a rock—or at least it appeared to be a rock. As his eyes focused, John realized the peculiar stone had decorative markings on it. Now curious, he scratched his head and blinked hard. He walked back and kicked the rock with his foot to dislodge it, but it was buried deeper than he expected. He bent down and clawed away at the surrounding dirt, thereby unearthing the strange artifact.

He held it in his soiled hand and rotated it. *What the hell is this?*

The stone was carved into the shape of a ball with graphic designs etched into it. He peered down at the hole he had dug and noticed the curved edge of another stone. He exhumed that one, only to see the edges of several more stone balls. He ran back to his car, grasped the rusted army shovel from the boot, and returned to the site. Eagerly, he dug up the field, unearthing thirteen stone balls, each featuring different etchings. John put them in his car and immediately drove three hours south to the National Museums Scotland, in Edinburgh.

Jim Brodie, the museum's curator, greeted John, and eagerly examined the stone balls. His eyes scrutinized each one closely. As he did, he placed three of them off to the side, then looked back at the group of ten. "These stone balls are in fine condition, Mr. Halford. We have in our collection about two hundred of these mysterious balls." His eyes drifted to the three balls he had placed off to the side. "However, these three are exquisite and quite unique. In fact, they are unlike any others ever found."

John squinted, still puzzled. "But what the hell are they?"

Mr. Brodie shrugged. "We don't know. They're one of those mysteries that have baffled scientists for many years."

That wasn't the response John wanted to hear. He was looking to cash in big, and that these rocks had no purpose put a big damper on his projected jackpot. "Well, do you at least know how old they are?"

Brodie nodded. "We believe they date back two to three thousand years BC."

John's eyes lit up. "Three *thousand* BC!" He gazed at the stone balls. "You mean to say these things are five thousand years old!?"

The curator smiled. "Yes. Most fascinating, isn't it? They're truly ancient works of art. If only we knew the meanings of these etched symbols."

The only symbol John saw now was the pound sterling symbol. "Yes! Most fascinating. So, how much would you be willing to pay for these?"

Brodie's enthusiasm wilted. "Ah, yes, I see our interpretation of *fascinating* differs somewhat. But yes, they also happen to be a lucrative find, Mr. Halford." His eyes surveyed the collection. "I'd say those ten are worth eight hundred pounds each, while those three... well, those three are worth quite a bit more."

John's face already beamed like a glowworm as he prodded, "What's *quite a bit more*? Like two thousand pounds each?" he goaded, aiming to push the envelope.

"No, no, not two thousand, Mr. Halford..." As John's face turned glum, Brodie continued, "I'd say more like five thousand pounds sterling. Each."

John swallowed a glorious lump of greed. Impulsively, he grabbed the three special balls and pushed the box of ten toward the curator. "Fine. I'll take the eight thousand pounds for those, and hold onto *these*."

The curator squinted. "Why won't you sell those three, Mr. Halford? They're the ones I'd want most."

"Exactly!" John said. "That's why I'll hold on to them. I'll bet their value will accrue in time and be worth ten or twenty thousand pounds each. Sound investments, Mr. Brodie, that's why."

The curator glanced at his new acquisitions. "Very well, have it your way, Mr. Halford. I'll gladly take these off your hands. I have a personal affinity for these mysterious stone balls. Most have been found right here in our country, you know. I suspect one day we'll discover what they were used for."

"Yeah, perhaps so," John said, as he discreetly rolled his eyes. *What an idiot, spending eight thousand pounds for* rocks, *stupid stones that don't even have a use. Only humans can be that stupid.*

As he waited for the transaction to be completed, a bald fat man, with a paper plate of strawberry shortcake in his hand and wearing thick glasses, approached him. "Excuse me, but I overheard your conversation," he said around a mouthful of cake. He chewed quickly and forced the cake down his hefty gullet. Licking the butter-cream off his crooked teeth, he went on, "I don't mean to pry, but I've been long fascinated with these mysterious stone balls. Would you mind if I take a closer look?"

John peered down at the stone balls in the box—which he now protectively cradled in his arms like gold bullion—then defensively stepped back. "What for? Are you a scientist or just some crazy fanatic?"

The chubby middle-aged man chuckled. "I suppose a bit of both, Mr. Halford."

"So you gleaned my name, as well, I see."

"Oh, excuse me," the man said, as he licked the paper plate clean and then threw the plastic fork and plate into the trash. "My name is Elmer Collins. I'm a geologist here at the museum." He licked his stubby fingers, then stuck out his hand. But John didn't shake. Elmer shrugged and wiped his moist mitts on his shirt as he went on. "I also handle all the electronics and IT, as well." He pushed his Coke-bottle glasses firmly up on the bridge of his nose, and added, "I guess you can say I'm the proverbial nerd."

As Elmer smiled, revealing his crooked teeth with traces of butter-cream and strawberries stuck between them, John slapped on a pseudo-smile while his mind belched: *No shit, Sherlock! Then again, you look more like a bald Benny Hill—a goofy comedian.*

John glanced down at the balls. "Sure, take a peek, Elmer. Perhaps *you* can tell me the truth."

Elmer squinted. "The truth?"

"That they're worth more than ten thousand pounds each, of course."

Elmer giggled. "You're a funny man, Mr. Halford. I heard our curator tell you five thousand each."

"Call me John. And go ahead. Take a look, a close look." He extended the box like a proud pirate showing off his stolen treasure. "There they are. Real beauties, aren't they?"

Elmer held the rim of his telescopic glasses as he examined each one closely. He glanced up at John. "Do you mind if I pick them up?"

"By all means. See for yourself how, uh... *exquisite* they are. Yeah! That's the word: exquisite. Even Jimbo, your curator, used that word."

"Indeed, they are," Elmer replied with a chuckle as he gingerly picked up two balls. Wholly intrigued, Elmer scrutinized their unusual etchings. "Jim was right," he said. "These *do* have very peculiar markings." He lifted, then lowered them in his meaty hands. "Dear me, and they're significantly lighter than any in our collection. I wonder what they're made of; they're unlike any stone ball we've ever seen. And believe me, Jim and I have seen at least five hundred of them."

"Five hundred? I thought he said you have two hundred?"

"Yes, we have the largest collection, John, but other museums have them, as well. And I've made an effort to examine all of them."

"Why?" John blurted. He shrugged. "I mean, seriously, why waste your time on stupid stones?"

Elmer shook his head as he placed the stones back in the box and stepped back. "You don't understand, Mr. Hal— uh, John. These stones are one of the world's greatest enigmas." He paused, pulled a ballpoint pen out of his pocket, then corrected, "Well, perhaps not *greatest*, but certainly one of the *oldest* enigmas. Their ages alone are simply mindboggling. More importantly, they had to be used for *something*. But what? Surely such well-crafted stones as these were not used as weapons, as they're all in very good condition. And if used as such, they would be marred with chips or various signs of distress. Yet that's not the case." As he continued, he clicked the ballpoint pen as if feeding his thoughts. "Could they have been religious artifacts? And if so, what significance do they hold? And for what purpose?" His magnified eyes behind his thick glasses rolled in thought. "Or were they simply used for a leisure game, like bocce or croquet?" His wandering eyes fixed on

John's. "All these questions feed my appetite to uncover the answer, Mr. Halford. And I would relish the opportunity to study these three fine artifacts at your home one day, if that's agreeable?"

Just then, a clerk walked out and issued John his check. John eagerly took hold of it, then looked back at Elmer. "Sure, why not. If you could uncover their purpose, I'm sure that would boost their value ten-fold. So by all means."

Elmer jotted his home phone number on the back of his museum business card and handed it to John. John shoved it in his pocket with the check, grabbed his precious stone balls, and exited the museum.

As he traveled back north, toward Aberdeen, turbulent gray clouds loomed on the horizon. The foreboding gloom intensified with each kilometer, as the dismal shroud choked the cerulean hues out of the sky. John finally made his way into town just as rain let loose. Impulsively, he turned and stopped at Tim's Tavern for a nightcap. He locked his MG Midget and ran through the rain into the pub. Only four familiar town locals were left sitting at the bar, and John ordered them all a round on the house.

Tim looked at him sternly. "Now ya can't be doin' that, John! Unless ya got the coin ta pay for it."

"No worries, old man, I got the dough, plenty of it. So shut up and give these boys another round," he retorted, as he shook the rain off himself like a dog.

John's four drinking partners nodded their thanks, while John stepped up and sat at the bar. "And I'll have my usual, Tim.... uh, in fact, never mind the cheap Chivas. Make it a Macallan Rare Cask!"

Tim looked at John like he had two heads. "Macallan Rare Cask? Are ya kiddin' me, man? That bottle cost me two hundred n' twenty pounds! You best have the coin, Johnny, otherwise I'll put ya *in* a rare cask*!*"

As the four men laughed, John snapped, "Shut your trap, you ornery old sod, and pour me a glass!"

As drinks were served and glasses and mugs clinked, a roar of violent thunder rattled the walls while lightning flashed through the tavern's tainted bay window.

As one fellow recoiled from the thunderclap, he exclaimed, "Now *that's* what I call one helluva round!"

"Indeed!" another said. "That shot went down with a bang, all right!"

Two hours later, the four men had left, while John sat at the bar savoring his sixth glass of Macallan Scotch. A silly smile was plastered on his face.

Tim washed the last dirty mug and slid the tab in front of John. "Okay, happy Halford, the pah-tee's over. Time ta pay up."

"Don't w-worry, old man. For Christ's s-sake!" John snapped with a slur. "You're ruinin' my cella-bration. I'll p-pay ya ta-morrow." Downing the last drop of Macallan, he slammed the glass down on the bar. "Shit Almighty, you old geezer! *I said* I'm good f-for it."

Tim's face turned crimson as his nostrils flared like a Spanish bull's. "I told ya, Johnny, this ain't no charity mill. But if yar lookin' for a shellackin', ya came ta the right place." Tim rolled up a newspaper and marched angrily toward him. John flinched and pulled the check out of his pocket, then waved it in Tim's face. "Hold on, old m-man! Calm d-down! Like I t-told ya. I got the mash."

Tim squinted, trying to focus on the check with his old, cataract-clad eyes. Once it came into view, however, his head jerked backward. "Why in blazes would a high-falutin' museum give a fop like *you* a dandy ol' check like *that*?"

John snarled at the insult and stuck the check back in his pocket. Yet when he thought about it, he looked up and giggled. "Well, Tiny Tim, I g-guess they just have *r-rocks* in their heads!" John laughed at his own witticism and added, "Or at least... r-rocks in their useless d-display. And I do mean *useless!*"

Tim was now even more confused. "Enuff with the mystree, John boy. *Why*?"

John chuckled. "It t-truly *is* a m-mystery, old man. I t-tell no lie. It's l-like all t-those idiots who b-bought pet r-rocks. M-makes no s-sense!" He pushed the empty glass of Macallan's toward Tim and rose from the stool. "Like I told ya, you'll get your bloody bangers. Once I c-cash that b-baby ta-morrow, I'll s-stop by and s-settle the score... with a n-nice t-tip for ya ta boot."

With that, John wobbled out the door, while Tim shook his head and turned off the lights.

John staggered to his car through the heavy rain and drove the two blocks to his disheveled apartment. He placed his box of goodies on the dinette table, then took the three stone balls out and placed them on the old, worn-out Formica surface. He sat down and gazed at them in wonder. *What the hell c-could you p-possibly be for?*

He picked one up and looked at it through his inebriated eyes. He glanced at the bills and summonses on the floor, then back at his precious stone and laughed. "But you and y-your ten b-buddies s-sure as hell got m-me out of a p-pickle." He scratched his head. "For a while, anyhow."

As he sat and gazed at the stone ball, thoughts of his beloved castle once again drenched his mind like the driving rain outside. He could feel his soul sinking into a soggy bog as visions of the castle's interior—which he had seen only in press photos—filled his mind: the grand staircase, the luxurious master bedroom, the ornate dining room, the numerous guestrooms and classy billiards room; all just tantalizing images of the extravagant lifestyle of luxury he was gypped out of and knew he'd never possess. He grasped the three stone balls and hugged them tightly, as if the castle he never had. Wearily, he slumped over them, as the Scotch weighed heavily on his mind. Soon, he was fast asleep.

Sometime later, John lifted his lazy eyelids, and slowly emerged from his slumber. He had no idea how long he'd nodded off. But once his lazy eyes focused, his whole body quaked. The stone balls were gone!

His eyes bulged as his head spun toward the door, then toward the windows, aiming to see if the flat was broken into. He ran to each, yet all were locked and no signs of a breach were found. No furniture was moved or drawers opened; *nothing* was amiss. Nervously, he shook his head, then peered down at the empty box.

Jesus Christ, John! What did you do with them? Try to remember, you drunken twit!

Anxiously he turned over the pillows on the couch, looked in all the drawers, under the bed; everywhere he could think of. But still, *nothing*! Anxiously, he shoved his hand into his pocket, searching for the check, then pulled it out of his pocket. He sighed. *Thank ya, Lord. At least this whole damn thing wasn't a dream.*

He gazed at the check, and tried to retrace his actions. But they all led to the same round of drinks at Tim's Tavern, then home. He pulled out Elmer Collin's business card from his pocket, then looked at the clock. It was only 2:30 AM. He shoved it back in his pocket; he'd have to wait until morning to call...

As the sun cascaded through his tiny apartment's windows, John blinked hard, his head still somewhat numb from the Scotch. Immediately, he remembered the missing balls and turned toward the dinette table, foolishly hoping they'd be there. His eyes bulged as he sprang to his feet and dashed over to the table. There, before his blurry eyes, were the three stone balls!

What the hell!? Was it the booze last night, or did I imagine them gone?

John picked up the three balls to make sure they were real. A goofy grin etched itself on his face. "Damn, am I happy to see you blokes! Where the hell did you go?"

He sat down and pondered his last sentence. *Yeah. Where did you go last night?*

He glanced around the flat, recalling that all the doors and windows had not been breached. He pulled out Elmer Collins' business card and quickly picked up the phone. Once Elmer answered, he gushed, "Elmer, it's John Halford. You must come over, *right away?* I need to speak with you about these weird stones."

Elmer chuckled. "*Weird?* Sure, John. Aberdeen is a bit of a hike from here, but I suppose I could be there in two or three hours, depending on traffic. But, what's the hurr—"

"Just make sure you bring a *complete* sampling kit!" John interrupted. "Do you hear me? I need to know more about these damn things, and *fast*. Is that understood?"

"Understood, John. But you seem a bit paranoid. What's going on?"

"Never mind, we'll speak when you get here," John said, and he hung up.

Bubbling with anticipation, John paced the small flat as he stared at the mysterious stones. His mind was in a knot as he tried to figure out what occurred. Two and a half hours later, Elmer arrived with his huge suitcase, and John escorted him to the rickety table. "Elmer, I want you to examine every damn facet of these balls, *right away*. They not only look different than the rest, but *act* different, as well."

Elmer once again chuckled. "John, they're *stones*. What do you mean *act*?"

John explained the odd occurrence, while Elmer just shrugged, not convinced of the odd tale, especially coming from a man who reeked of Scotch. Yet, Elmer had been eager from the start to examine the stones' physical compositions, so without further ado, he set to work.

The hefty scientist bent over, with the stressed groan of a hippo in labor, and opened his equally large suitcase. Diligently, Elmer set up his apparatus on the table and quickly turned toward the specimens. He scratched a small sample off of each of the stones' surfaces and placed them under the microscope. Forty minutes later, after running a series of tests, Elmer looked up at Halford, baffled. "I'm at a loss for words, John. These stones seem to have no Earthly properties whatsoever." He adjusted his thick glasses with his short stubby fingers and gazed pensively at the stones.

Meanwhile, John moved closer and picked one up. He tossed it a few inches straight up and caught it, like a softball. "I knew it!" he said with a grin. "I just knew these things would be worth a fortune!"

Elmer gazed at John, bewildered, not sure if he should pity him or persecute him for his petty display of greed. "John! I don't think you grasp the full gravity of what I just said. These stones are *not from this planet*. They are some form of alien material, unknown to mankind. These must be studied by a diverse group of scientists from all fields, because they—"

"Never mind that!" John snapped. "*I* found them, and

I own them." He paused briefly, then added, "At some point, I *might* allow them to be studied, but I have other plans."

Elmer heatedly crossed his milky-white flabby arms. "Other plans, John? Like what, exactly?"

"Like, I want you to install a video camera in one of them."

"A *camera*?" Elmer belched. "What in God's name for?"

John looked at the nerd before him—wearing his long-white lab coat and thick glasses—and snickered. "You see, eggheads like *you* piss away countless hours, months, and years behind locked doors taking samples and doing your typical data-collecting bullshit. But I thought *beyond* the laboratory. If you listened, Elmer, I said these stones *disappeared* last night, then *returned* this morning. They went *somewhere*. And I intend to find out where."

Elmer placed his chubby hands on his hefty hips and rolled his eyes. "Okay, even if I believe your wild tale, John—that they somehow disappeared and reappeared—tell me; how do you intend to activate their launch? Do you have a special phrase or word, like *Abracadabra*?"

John grasped Elmer's meaty hand and placed the stone ball firmly in it. "Don't be silly, Humpty Dumpty! I'm not kidding when I said they traveled somewhere." John peered deeply into Elmer's eyes. "I suspect that the electrical storm last night had something to do with it, along with my thoughts."

"Oooo…kay," Elmer said condescendingly. "So now you're saying that you *willed* these balls to go somewhere?" Unexpectedly, he laughed. "That's delightful!"

"Look, Tubby! It *is* possible," John retorted. As Elmer's face twitched at the growing insults and turned solemn, John continued, "Let's face it; they've been sitting in the dirt for thousands of years with no activity. Right? They've endured countless electrical storms, and still, no activation. Right? Yet when I fell asleep holding them—consumed with thoughts about my castle—they managed to activate and disappear. So, Mr. *Brilliant* Egghead, how do you explain *that*?"

Elmer shrugged and remained mute as he struggled to stifle the laughter that reverberated inside his massive egg-shaped, bald dome.

Meanwhile, John smirked. "Listen, I know it sounds far-fetched, but so, too, is the fact that these stone balls are not from planet Earth. Who the hell would believe *that*?"

"Well, John," Elmer reasoned, "they could be small meteors."

John snorted with a snigger. "Oh, sure; meteors that are carved into perfectly round balls with intricate designs etched on them?"

Elmer's hefty shoulders sunk with embarrassment. "Okay, I spoke before thinking." He rubbed his double chin. "This idea of yours still sounds crazy, but fine. I can imbed a small video camera into it with a memory card that will hold plenty of footage. This way, when it returns, we can see exactly where it went."

"Excellent! Now you're talking."

Elmer paused as a wave of concern marred his fleshy face. "But what if these things travel back to their home planet... and... what if the aliens don't like that we turned them into spy-drones?"

John nonchalantly waved his hand. "You watch too many Sci-Fi flicks, Elmer. If an alien race made these, remember, they've been sitting here for thousands of years, doing *nothing*, forgotten. Nobody wants them anymore, except your museum and myself. And I have plans. *Big* plans. So if this test flight works, we'll see what happens."

Two days later, Elmer returned to deliver one stone ball with a video camera and memory card embedded, as promised. He even gave John one of his new laptops with access to the Internet, which had recently grown into a worldwide web. Elmer also warned John about the Y2K threat that might wreak havoc across the globe in the coming year.

As the days passed, John waited anxiously for another thunderstorm. It dawned on him that if his theory was correct, the alien balls had landed in an ideal location, as the heavy rains and electrical storms of Scotland provided the perfect environment to charge and activate them.

A week went by as John impatiently paced to and fro in his small flat, gazing irritably out the window, up at the clear blue sky. His waning patience and growing anticipation consumed him. Visions of the new doorways that would open up for him and his miserable life—if this experiment panned out—fueled the adrenaline that raced through his pulsating veins.

Meanwhile, back in Edinburgh, Elmer's reservations and fears had grown. Poor Elmer was having visions of waking up to see a Death Star hovering in the stratosphere, while stormtroopers raided Scotland's bucolic countryside. Their mission: to find the culprits who had attempted to spy on them.

Two days later, however, storm clouds gathered. As electrical charges snapped and ripped through the sky, John sat at his shabby dinette table, eagerly clutching the stone balls. It was time to condition his mind for the metaphysical journey. He had scoured several books about the Craigievar Castle and was ready. He closed his eyes tight, and envisioned the construction of the castle in 1626. He realized his scheme was crazy, but finding alien stone balls had even been crazier. So, as he figured it, *anything* was possible.

The sky illuminated with electricity as lightning rummaged through the heavens. With his eyes still shut, John could feel a tingling sensation in his hands. It appeared as if the stone balls were getting warm, yet he wasn't sure; was it his nervous hands and vivid imagination, or the stones? All at once, the alien balls glowed with static electricity, then vanished! Startled, John's eyes sprang open as he pushed himself away from the table—a grin gracing his face. Excitedly, he leapt to his feet and called Elmer: "The Three Musketeers have taken flight!"

Elmer wasn't sure if he should rejoice or repent.

Filled with dread, Elmer said little, then hung up. His mind reeled, *could this madman be right? Or is he pulling my leg?*

Elmer made a hot cup of tea and tried to read a book to divert his attention, but his mind kept returning to the eerie event. They must have disappeared, he figured. The possible rewards or deadly ramifications of this miraculous event chilled him to the bone. As poor Elmer had a restless night, John managed to down a beer, then contentedly dozed off.

At daybreak, John woke to see the three stone balls sitting peacefully on his dinette table. He ran over and picked up the ball with the camera. He pulled out the memory card and slipped it into Elmer's laptop. He clicked on the mpeg file, and *voilà*! The video stuttered for a second or two, then played like a charm. John rubbed his nubby, dropped jaw as he watched the stone drone swoop down toward the unfinished castle. Down below, workers in baroque-styled clothing with antiquated tools were putting the finishing touches on the towering, pink structure.

John blinked twice, to see if the vision was real or an illusion. He had fervently hoped this insane anomaly would come to fruition, but seeing the past captured in live footage, and in full color, was overwhelming.

He shouted, "YES! YES! YES!" as he punched the air.

John's covetous eyes couldn't stop staring at his beloved castle, as the drone made several more passes around it. A mischievous glint emanated from John's eyes, as he rubbed his hands together. "Now for sure, you *will* be mine, my sweet Craigievar!"

Three hours later, Elmer arrived. With relief, the nervous geek finally giggled his fears away, as he cheered, "It's incredible! You did it, John! You performed a miracle!"

John looked at him calmly, confidently. "No, Elmer, the *real* miracle has yet to commence, *after* you install an explosive in one of the other balls."

Elmer gasped. "An *explosive!*? What are you talking about? For what?"

"That's none of your business, Elmer," John snapped. "These are *my* stone balls— until, that is, I decide to sell them to your museum." John patted the balls. "Now, you *do* want credit for presenting these alien specimens to your curator *and* the world, don't you?"

Elmer's nerves tingled with trepidation once again as he adjusted his thick glasses, trying to decipher what was going on in John Halford's warped mind. But he came up blank. So he had to ask. "Just what are you planning, John? If it's anything like going back in time to kill Hitler or Stalin, that's just foolhardy. We can never guess what ramifications that would have on world events." Just the thought of it made Elmer queasy, as he wiped his sweaty brow. "Consider this, John: the research and development of rockets, atomic energy, and computers might never have happened without the harrowing events of World War Two. And... and, well, you and I, John... might never have been born."

John shook his head reassuringly. "Don't worry that pork-butt head of yours, Elmer Fudd. I have no intentions of tinkering with world history. Now, will you install an explosive in one of these balls, or do I call someone else? And if I do, I *will* sell these stone balls to another museum, and your glorious road to fame will turn into a detour, one that leads to a dead end. Do I make myself clear?"

Elmer meekly lowered his head. "You're not a nice person, John Halford."

"I never claimed to be. But I *am* a regal person, a potential baron who was robbed of his estate and lofty life by some queer misfit." The animosity that brewed in John's gut now burned like lava, and he couldn't help but spew the flaming vitriol: "My bigshot cousin, William Forbes, died in 1965, Elmer, which transferred ownership of the estate to his sibling, Ewan. But get this: Ewan had been born *and* documented as *Elizabeth*." As Elmer squinted, John continued, "Yes, Elizabeth. She was born a female, Elmer, and lived as a woman for forty years! Therefore, she was *not* entitled to the male-line inheritance stipulated in our baronetcy, regardless of changing her name *or* sex in 1952."

Elmer stood in shock, as John's wrath continued: "So if I kill William Forbes *before* that genetic freak changes her name and sex, Craigievar Castle and the baronetcy will go to *me*, the next male heir in line! The *rightful* heir! *Now* do you understand?"

Elmer could feel the sweat trickling down his fat, hairy back as he looked at John's maniacal eyes and animated gestures. He had doubts about John's sanity, not to mention abhorring his crude remarks about his transgender cousin. But being the meek man that he was, Elmer knew he hadn't the will or the strength to overpower the raging lunatic before him. Furthermore, the lure of gaining possession of this earth-shattering find for his museum would indeed be the windfall of the century. After all, Elmer knew every scientist secretly yearned to be recognized, or even lionized, for something monumental. So even if he were to be a footnote in the grand story of this mega-milestone, his seemingly provincial life would be elevated and enshrined in the history books for all time.

More pressing at the moment, however, was that Elmer knew that if he didn't help John now, someone else would. So why throw it all away? Nevertheless, Elmer was deeply troubled by one last question: namely, the killing of an innocent man.

"Listen, J-John," he stuttered while nervously rubbing his thick lips. "I s-sort of understand your motives, but how do you have the nerve to k-kill someone... your c-cousin, no less?"

John opened a drawer and pulled out several old newspaper clippings. Each featured articles of how William Forbes was a decorated fighter pilot in both the First and Second World Wars. Elmer grasped the clippings and peered down at them. As he skimmed through the spectacular headlines his stomach turned, becoming even more repulsed by John's dastardly scheme. *What the hell is he thinking?* Elmer thought as his heart raced and hands trembled.

John stared at Elmer with a deadpan face as he pulled out several other clippings and handed them to him.

With his stomach still in knots, Elmer dreaded reading more, but he forced himself to read on. His eyes then caught hold of one article that caused him to recoil. Evidently, William Forbes had passed secret information on to the Japanese, being reprimanded by Winston Churchill, who derided and branded him as a treacherous spy. Elmer's eyes then caught another article, this one revealing that Forbes was an ardent admirer of Adolf Hitler and the Nazi Party, in addition to being a fervent anti-Semite.

Elmer's tense stomach subsided as his erratic heartbeat regained its rhythm. His mind raced with thoughts as it resurrected fragments of his youth. His dearly departed mother, Hilda, had been German. She, like many others, had fled Nazi Germany in 1933, once Hitler became Reich Chancellor. She had often drilled into Elmer's young head a recurring refrain; namely, how critical it was for Western civilization to survive during those hellish years, and how all those who stood firmly behind Hitler—who viewed all others as subhuman parasites—were, in fact, the true vermin of the Earth.

The clippings fell by Elmer's side as he irritably whacked them against his hefty thigh. He pushed his glasses firmly up against the bridge of his nose, then looked up at John. "So, William turned out to be a villain...a disgrace to Scotland *and* the Allies."

"Exactly," John replied with a sense of vindication. "So why should I feel an ounce of remorse for killing a traitor? Never mind the fact that—when my parents died during the war—he and his family shunned me, as if I were garbage. In a bad twist of fate, I became like Oliver Twist, alone and left to fend for myself. My nobleman's heritage had been reduced to the grimy status of an orphaned pauper." Through gritted teeth he added, "I was robbed!"

Elmer glanced at Halford's shanty apartment—the life he was unfairly relegated to—then at the three stone balls; John's only hope for reclaiming what was rightfully his. Empathetically, he looked back at John. "Okay, fine," Elmer relented. "I'll help you. But this is the last time I do anything of this sort. You *must* agree to sell these three balls to my museum and ensure that *I* get sole credit for uncovering their alien nature."

John nodded with a smile; knowing that Elmer's yearning for fame was the added ingredient necessary to pull this scheme off.

With that, Elmer reluctantly fulfilled his end of the bargain and installed an explosive mechanism in one of the stone balls, specially crafted to Halford's curious specifications. Namely, it was configured to home in on a specific metallic object—not made of iron or steel, but rather duralumin—and detonate.

With the stage set, John and Elmer waited for a storm. As the days passed, Elmer once again found himself plagued with reservations. His mind wondered: *Did I sell my soul to a devil, a devil hell-bent on murdering his cousin, just to gain the castle and estate he felt cheated out of?*

Despite Elmer's indecision, the day had arrived, as storm clouds twisted the sky into ominous knots and choked the last remnants of daylight out of the sky.

Meanwhile, John sat eagerly at his rickety dinette table and hugged the three balls with a zeal and elation he hadn't known his entire, miserable life. He buried his mind deep into his dark, vengeful scheme, as he envisioned the day, in 1933, when his cousin William had flown on the famous Graf Zeppelin. The rigid airship, made of duralumin, had been the first commercial transatlantic fight service in the world, and had operated successfully, without incident, for nine years. John knew that very soon he'd be destroying that impressive record, but, as he figured it, it was a hydrogen-filled balloon. Therefore, it was only a matter of time before the Hindenburg disaster would put an end to such floating, metal dinosaurs anyhow.

John took a deep breath, closed his eyes, and immersed himself into his dream-wish. His concentration was so intense and so transcendent that he felt as if a spiritual awakening was lifting his soul. As thunder and lightning ripped through the skies, John could feel his hands starting to tingle. Suddenly, the balls grew warmer, then started to vibrate. With each tremor, John could feel his heart skipping another beat; until, finally, the three balls vanished!

John's eyes sprang open as he leapt to his feet and punched the air in victory. "YES! Do your dirty deeds, my precious trio!"

He paced to and fro, unable to contain the thrill that ran through his blood—his *aristocratic* blood! Soon, he would be the proud baron of Craigievar Castle and the esteemed estate he had pined for his entire life. John looked in the mirror. He felt like a king, or at least a king of his own castle. "*Sir* John Halford,' he said, "you *must* celebrate your upcoming coronation!"

He cracked open a bottle of Macallan Rare Cask—bought specifically for this regal occasion—and clutched a glass. His hand tipped the bottle forward, but then retracted, opting to dispense with formality. He was never one much for pomp and circumstance. John raised the bottle to his lips and took a healthy swig, then another, and another.

An hour later, he threw back his head to savor the last drop of Macallan, which trickled down his throat like liquid gold. With his pricey lubricant expended, John was about to grab a bottle of his usual Chivas, when the doorbell rang. He looked at the time: it was 11:30 PM. John reached for the handle and opened the door.

Elmer Collins rushed inside, soaking wet. "You didn't send them off already, did you!?"

John's liquored tongue enunciated his sardonic reply. "Of c-course I did, you f-fat fool! Why wouldn't I?"

Elmer gritted his teeth and tried to muster up the confidence he'd practiced in the car on the way over, as he finally spat, "I, I changed my mind! That's why. You can't murder your cousin, John!" Taking off his hat and snapping the rain off of it, he continued, "And I just figured out why you wanted the bomb to home-in on duralumin—you plan to blow up a Zeppelin! You're mad! Do you hear me? Mad! You'll also kill innocent people on that flight, and I won't be a party to this!"

"You already j-joined the party, you blabbering blimp," John retorted as he slammed the door closed on the torrential rain. "We s-settled on an agreement—*a deal.* Remember? And I intend to k-keep my end of the b-bargain, Porky. So s-shut up and wait for the Three Musketeers to r-return." He glanced at his watch. "They'll b-be here in a few hours."

"I said NO!" Elmer bellowed with a vim and vigor he never knew he had. "I'm going to call the police!" With that, Elmer pulled out his cell phone and started to dial nine-nine-nine—

He managed only the second digit before a loud crash echoed. Elmer fell to the floor with blood gushing out of his left ear and neck. Meanwhile, John stood over him with wide eyes—in his hands, a smashed bottle of Macallan Rare Cask, its jagged edges laced with blood. "*Oh shit!*" John belched. "Now look w-what you m-made me do, you f-fat bastard!" Angrily, he kicked Elmer's prostrate body and cussed, "You piece of s-shit! Get up! You'll ruin my p-plan, you p-pig bastard!"

But it was too late; Elmer was dead, his carotid artery sliced.

John kicked the carcass again, harder. "You p-piece of s-shit! You had to die on me, right?"

His inebriated eyes rolled as remedial thoughts flashed through his soggy head. Intuitively, he dragged Elmer's limp body into the bathroom, then heaved it into the tub. As Elmer's blood swirled down the drain, John diligently mopped up all the floors. He then bagged Elmer's body in a tarpaulin, along with the broken bottle, and hauled it out into the driving rain toward his MG Midget.

Drunk and out of breath, John keeled over and vomited; not so much from the thought of homicide as from the physical agitation of the liquor in his gut. Having caught his breath, he then lifted the hefty carcass and struggled to stuff it in the rear boot of the car. But the bulky mass wouldn't fit. John snarled as he jumped on Elmer's bagged body several times, aiming to compact it into the Midget's small compartment. On the last knee-drop, the plastic bag split open and the jagged bottle ripped through, exposing the torn label *Rare Cask*.

John snickered. "Rare cask, indeed, you fat bastard! Rest in peace, you piece of shit!"

He pressed down hard on the trunk lid and finally heard the latch snap closed. He slipped behind the wheel and drove through the raging storm in the black of night. He pushed the old Midget up to eighty kilometers per hour and traveled across country to Loch Ness. He hopped out into the driving rain and scanned the hilly terrain. It was dark and eerily vacant as a thick fog wafted across the lake. He opened the boot and struggled to unload the hefty parcel, which fell to the ground with a thud. "You fat piece of shit!" he spat, "You couldn't be a lightweight and made my life easier, right?"

With that, John dragged the weighted mass by the feet and hurled it over the edge. He kicked the bagged body out into the rapid current, and waited for it to sink. He smiled. *Maybe Nessie will eat it, eh?*

Some three hours later, John returned to Aberdeen just as daylight scratched the horizon. By the time he walked in the door, it was 6 AM. As he ripped off his raincoat, his eyes immediately zeroed in on the dinette table. But there was no sign of the stone balls.

Dumbfounded, he rubbed his weary head and slouched on the sofa. He gazed into space as his mind twisted and growled. He was pissed. Elmer—the blubbery nuisance—had thrown a wrench into his grand scheme. Yet as he contemplated Elmer's weighted body sinking to the depths of Loch Ness, it dawned on him: Despite how huge Elmer was, even Nessie, the enormous sea monster, had never been found. His plan was brilliant! With a sigh and a giggle, John's mind returned to his pending future, with all its luxurious trappings.

He gazed at the vacant dinette table, then back at the clock: a monotonous routine that consumed him over the next ten hours as he shook his head and wondered *What the hell happened? Where are you, damn it?*

A moment later, his head sprang up. *Of course!*

He pulled out Elmer's laptop and fired it up. Impatiently, he clicked the icon to open the web browser, then searched for "William Forbes." The screen illuminated with a biographical article, replete with photos. John eagerly scrolled down, and there it was!... a bold headline from 1933. It brought a grin to his face.

"Baron William Forbes Dies Tragically Today Aboard the Graf Zeppelin."

Below that the text read:

"The enormous metal airship mysteriously exploded at 7:32 PM while attempting to land. Several eyewitnesses claimed to have seen some type of small projectile fly into the vessel. That is when a devastating fireball erupted, igniting the huge, hydrogen-filled airship. Many suspect sabotage, but no tangible evidence has materialized."

John scrolled farther down and landed on a later article: "The Legacy of The Forbes Estate." Underneath that, it read:

"William's only surviving sibling was his sister Elizabeth. Under the terms of the estate, Craigievar Castle and all of the family's holdings were transferred to William's first cousin, Sir John Halford."

John covered his mouth to contain his exhilaration. With his hands starting to tremble, he continued reading:

"Despite legal claims made some twenty years later by Elizabeth—who had by then changed her name to Ewan and her sex to male—the courts ruled in favor of Sir John Halford, who remains the owner of the majestic estate and historic castle."

John unclasped his mouth and bellowed: "Yeah, baby! I did it! I'm rich! The castle is all mine. Mine! Mine! Mine!"

He tossed the laptop on the sofa and dashed to the liquor cabinet. He pulled out a bottle of Chivas and cracked it open. He was about to take a swig, when the doorbell rang. Nervously, he scanned the floor where Elmer's blood had been. It was clean. Everything had been thoroughly sterilized or removed. Even the broken-glass weapon had been dumped with the body into the depths of Loch Ness. Nothing could possibly link him to the murder. Confidently, John marched to the door and opened it.

A construction salesman stood before him with a faux smile. "Greetings, Sir Halford. You're a hard man to track down, but it's an honor to meet you. Do you have a moment?"

John rolled his eyes and huffed. "For what?"

"To discuss renovating your castle, naturally."

John smirked as he glanced at his bottle of Scotch. He wanted to get back to celebrating. Again, he huffed. "Why the hell would I want to do *that*?"

The man's painted smile withered as a look of bewilderment came over him. "Surely you must know how badly the castle has fallen into disrepair, Sir Halford. You haven't invested a penny into maintaining it since you inherited it back in 1933. I know you were only two years old at the time, but after your governors maintained it until you were of age, you never paid much heed to your the estate," he hesitated, "or perhaps the rumors of your reckless spending may account for it."

John's eyebrows pinched. He hadn't given much thought to all the years in-between, from his inheritance until now. The hangover from the previous night's drink-fest and Elmer's blood-fest now truly rattled his head.

Meanwhile, the man continued, "Anyhow, It's been well publicized that your castle needs extensive renovation, as sixty-percent of it has deteriorated. I don't know what your current financial situation is, Sir Halford, but there are many noble and royal families that have fallen upon hard times, and my company does offer zero-percent financing."

John's mind was a battlefield of conflicting thoughts, but he couldn't believe a word this idiot had to say, as his now-flaming eyes bore holes into the man's head. "I don't need your zero-percent financing, you jackass! And I have *not* fallen upon hard times. I fell upon a *gold mine*. I'm rich, you moron. I'm a baron. I'm nobility! Now get the hell out of here, you money-hungry leech!"

John slammed the door in his face as disturbing thoughts clouded his brain. *Shit! Did I mismanage my estate all these years?* He glanced around his disheveled flat, a reflection of the mismanaged life he had led as a pauper. He shook his head, not wanting to believe it, but then his eyes lit up. He turned and darted to the laptop, this time to search for his own name.

As "John Halford" came up on Wikipedia, he quickly perused the page, and his eyes landed on a disturbing paragraph:

"Ever since inheriting the estate, at the age of two, Sir John Halford failed to engage a financial advisor or administrative team to oversee the estate or invest the family's wealth. In 1943, the estate fell into bankruptcy and hasn't managed to recoup. Since then, the once dignified Craigievar Castle deteriorated. Today it sits amid several-decades' worth of rubble and weeds, in utter ruin."

John's eyes gazed at the depressing photo. His cherished castle was in shambles. His heart dropped. The image looked like Dresden after World War Two. Parts of the castle had collapsed, while its once pristine and smooth harled finish had peeled and blistered. A tear welled in his eye, when suddenly the phone rang.

He pulled his cell phone out of his pocket. "Hello," he mumbled. "Who is it?"

A firm voice rang out: "I believe you know who this is, Sir Halford. We've been trying to hunt you down for years. You owe fifty-three years of back taxes, Sir John, amounting to two million, six hundred thousand pounds, not including penalties. However, we do have several ways for you to pay off this immense deb—"

John threw the phone across the room as his angry, red face turned white, like an albino's. He gazed into space, numb, then blinked hard. He dashed out the door, looking for his MG Midget, but found a run-down 1934 Rolls Royce with rusted fenders instead. It was a remnant from the brief period when the estate had money, before it was devoured by taxes or unwisely spent.

John dug into his pocket and pulled out his keys: they were Rolls Royce keys. He hopped in, slammed the shift lever into gear, and drove through the hilly countryside for forty-five minutes, arriving in Alford. As he approached the castle, the wheels of the Rolls Royce crunched their way over the tall weeds and small bits of debris. A lump welled in his throat as he heatedly slammed the car into park and turned off the ignition. He leaned on the steering wheel and gazed mournfully at the decrepit castle through the pitted windshield of the rusted old Rolls.

A tear streamed down his cheek as he stepped out and limped his way over to the castle's front entrance. He pushed open the rotted wood door and stepped inside. The musty smell caused him to gag as he navigated through the deteriorated complex. He stopped and gazed at the ornate fireplace in the once Grand Hall, which now was cracked and missing large chunks of the rearing stone lion's head and legs. Cobwebs and dust draped all the rooms, evoking a macabre specter of death and decay as he made his way up the winding flights of stairs to the rooftop.

He rubbed his throbbing head and drew in a huge breath of fresh air, then expelled it, relieved to clear his lungs of the mold-infested air. Somberly, he lumbered his way over to the balustrade, where he rested his elbows and gazed out over the large estate. It was overgrown with weeds and splattered with dank, mosquito-infested bogs. The horrid stench matched the visually depressing swampland. His heart dropped. His life-long quest for nobility, riches, and his precious castle were for naught.

Yet as twilight descended on the grim estate, John was suddenly jolted by a chilling sound...a sound he knew. It was Elmer's pig-like screech! Startled, he looked down and saw a horrifying sight; a dark brown figure was weaving its way through the tall weeds! Thoughts of Elmer stuffed in the brown garbage bag came back with a vengeance. John spat, "You fat bastard, I killed you! How the hell could you have survived? Go away! Leave me alone!" With that, he leaned forward to get a closer look, when the rotted balustrade broke and Sir John Halford plunged seven stories to his death—his limp corpse lying mangled among the rotting refuse and weeds.

Out of the tall brush, a brown warthog wobbled its way toward the carcass, sniffed it, then continued on its way, as its snorts and squeals echoed into the dreary night.

A week later, John Halford's dead body was found, and, over the ensuing months, the National Trust for Scotland regained control of the defunct castle and the estate. The castle was handsomely renovated and successfully turned into a museum. Meanwhile, no mention of the mysterious stone balls of Aberdeen was ever made... until now.

— The End —

SPECIAL NOTE: This tale of fiction was based upon several true facts: namely, William Forbes and his transgender sibling Ewan/Elizabeth were real people of Scottish nobility. As noted, William was a famous aviator and notorious traitor, and did travel on the Graf Zeppelin, which did *not* mysteriously explode, however. Their Craigievar Castle, as shown in the illustration, was indeed given to the National Trust for Scotland and still exists to this day as a museum.

John Halford, Elmer Collins, and all other persons mentioned herein, are fictitious characters, as is the Sci-Fi plot. Meanwhile, the mysterious Scottish stone balls, dating from 3000 BC, do exist. However they are simply made of stone, not alien materials, and their use to this day still remains a mystery. I, the author, simply took the liberty of putting them to good use, or rather nefarious use!

DARK SIDE OF THE MOON

The savory smell of Angus burgers wafted in the air of astroengineer—and soon-to-be astronaut—Bobby Blake's backyard, as they sizzled on the grill.

Sitting at a wicker table on the Trex deck, his three older crewmembers talked shop and laughed as they drank their lemonades and iced teas. Meanwhile, their wives and husband downed martinis or beer, hoping to deaden their anxiety about their loved ones' flight tomorrow.

On their weary minds was the *Stepping Stone* lunar mission—conceived of and designed by wunderkind, Bobby Blake. The mission was being widely touted as humankind's first attempt to build a space station on the moon: a jumping point for future manned missions to Mars and beyond. Their SS-1 mission entailed installing the first section of what would take a total of ten consecutive flights to assemble the Stepping Stone Station, or S^3.

Bobby flipped the burgers, then pressed down on them, as the flames reared up like fiery dragons to lick the fatty juices. With an amorous smile, Bobby turned and pulled his wife, Suzy, in for an ardent kiss. As they did, flight mechanic Eddie Hasselberg sardonically cooed, "Aww, how sweet. The newlyweds are the perfect picture of young love. Aren't they?"

Sheila Sanders, the flight geologist, cocked her head toward Eddie and jabbed, "You're just jealous, Eddie, because they're sizzling hot, like that grill, and your wife tells me you're as cold as a refrigerator."

Eddie snickered as he gazed at his wife, Joanne. "So, now you're telling my crewmates about our sex life?"

Joanne rolled her eyes as she refreshed her chocolate martini. "Come off it, Eddie. Everyone here knows you're a cold fish!"

"So why the hell did you marry me?"

Joanne huffed. "I guess because I love sushi."

As they all laughed—except Eddie—Colonel Harold Zimmer, the flight commander, smirked. He was well acquainted with the couple's squabbles, and opted to divert the conversation back to the young and vibrant couple, as he raised his glass of lemonade. "I salute the lovely newlyweds! Your future trajectory will clearly go beyond the moon." As they all applauded, he added, "And thanks for throwing this splendid send-off party."

"Here, here!" Sheila cheered, as others echoed her salute.

As they all raised their glasses, Zimmer continued, "It's too bad you kids didn't get to go on your honey-*moon*." He glanced at Suzy. "But once Bobby returns from the moon, where will you lovebirds go?"

Bobby and Suzy's eyes connected with deep and fervent passion while their magnetic grins glistened in the evening light, like fireflies, all aglow. Bobby gazed back at his commander. "We're thinking of someplace bustling with people and alive with action, like Vegas, or possibly somewhere nostalgic, like Paris." Looking up at the moon, he added, "I mean, after spending four weeks in space on that desolate satellite, I figure I'll be yearning for a crowd of people."

They all toasted to the young couple and took sips of their drinks, except for Eddie, who continued scrolling through *Popular Mechanics* on his smart phone and, without looking up, said, "Hell, I love solitude. Just give me a car engine to rip apart and rebuild or my Cessna 172 Skyhawk to tinker with, and I'm a happy camper."

"Yes, Eddie," Joanne moaned, as she stirred her martini with her finger, then licked it clean. "We all know machined metal parts attract you more than flesh and blood. That's why after twenty-two years of marriage, we never had kids."

Eddie glared at Joanne. "Well, if I wasn't so obsessed and good at what I do, *sweetie*, I'd never have been chosen to fly on this important mission. So, there's the tradeoff. I prefer to dedicate myself to advancing science and human history, not being just another dull dad among billions."

The bon voyage party became uncomfortably quiet, as Joanne responded with a slight slur, "How can you c-compare flying a mission to a stupid asteroid to the truly m-miraculous act of g-giving birth?" Downing another large swig of her chocolate martini, her fifth of the evening, she added, "And how is it t-that the S-Sanders and Zimmers both have kids?" she said with a more pronounced slur. "Colonel Zimmer was a m-marine who defended our nation in Afghanistan and S-Syria, and is the commander of your s-ship. Yet *he* managed to have f-four kids. Is *he* a nobody or a d-dull dad?"

An uncomfortable wave permeated the group like pernicious gamma rays. As each glanced at their neighbor, Colonel Zimmer finally spoke up. "Let's not get into comparisons, Joanne. We each have our own separate lives, and none of us should pass judgment. I appreciate your acknowledgments, but personally, I don't need to know what your domestic gripes are. My main concern is our mission tomorrow. And my crew cannot have any emotional baggage onboard that might jeopardize the mission. We all need to be thinking clearly, with our minds focused on our tasks in space, not on our Earthly problems. You can address that in private when we return."

Joanne's lips twisted as she took another gulp of her martini, then spat. "Listen, Commander. You m-may be the b-boss of *their* flight, but you're n-not *my* boss!" With the liquor lubricating her languid tongue, she rattled on, "Maybe you w-were in the Middle East too long and acquired their m-misogynistic w-ways, but we're in America now. And I can s-say w-whatever the hell I want... Wherever I want... And w-whenever I want! Got t-that, Command-O Patton?"

Colonel Zimmer stood up and said, "SS-1 crew, make sure you get to bed early. I'll see you at the pad at six a.m. Have a good night." With that, he gently tapped on his wife's hand, and they left.

A dark cloud hung over the tense silence for several odd minutes, until Bobby said, "Okay, so how do you all like your burgers? Medium? Rare? Well done?" Facing them all, he added with a grin, "Or Well-burned? Like this party!"

As they all chuckled, except Joanne, they gathered their rolls and condiments and filled their plates with coleslaw, baked beans, and French fries.

†††

At six the next morning, all SS-1 crewmembers arrived at Cape Canaveral on time. Bobby strolled in wearing his running shorts and sneakers, having just finished his routine ten-mile morning run. As they each suited up and proficiently ran through their checklists, not a word was mentioned about last night's awkward debacle.

Packed and ready, the flight crew walked toward the towering gantry. As their eyes all glanced up at the colossal, 650-foot tall spacecraft, Colonel Zimmer edged closer to Bobby and whispered, "My apologies for missing your burgers last night, especially since you know how much I love them."

Bobby nodded discreetly as they both stepped into the elevator. "No problem, sir. Under the circumstances, you did the right thing. Perhaps not as a hardnosed commander, like Patton, but certainly as a fine gentleman. I'm just glad you didn't smack her!" As Zimmer chuckled, Bobby added, "I'm honored to serve with you, Colonel."

"Thank you, Blake. I believe a good commander must know which battles are worth fighting, and which are best to avoid."

Meanwhile, Eddie bumped into Sheila as he squeezed through the elevator gate ahead of her. As Sheila entered and rolled her eyes, Eddie said, "What's the look for? You women fought for over a century to be called *equal*, so deal with it, like a man!" He cracked his neck like a prizefighter. "In case you didn't get the memo, Sheila, chivalry is dead."

37

"Yes, but that doesn't mean *courtesy* is dead," she retorted as the elevator gate slid shut.

While the elevator started to ascend, Zimmer, once again, opted to divert the conversation. "Anyhow, I'm honored to have a Texas A&M's *summa cum laude* astroengineer aboard this flight." As Eddie and Sheila glanced at Blake and offered a wink and a nod, Zimmer added, "But I must ask, how the hell does a twenty-eight-year old kid design a complex lunar space station?"

Having reached the top, Bobby slid open the gate, then turned back and smiled. "Actually, I'm a bit slow, Colonel." He stepped out and opened the capsule's main hatch. "Einstein developed his theory of relativity at age twenty-six."

With a look of surprise on each of the three astronauts' faces, they followed Blake into the capsule, took their seats, and strapped themselves in, as they eagerly waited for the technicians to complete the checklist.

An hour later, the countdown began: ten, nine, eight, seven, six, five...

On the sound of "four," they felt the huge thrusters ignite. The massive ship vibrated violently, along with their bodies, and by the final count of "zero," the pneumatic and electrical umbilical cords broke free, while the restraining clamps finally released the ship. With a hefty jolt, the SS-1 lifted off the pad. Its tremendous nine engines emitted long, fiery trails, while furious billows of smoke mushroomed into the dawning sky.

Spectators stood in awe as they watched the massive ship—almost twice the size of the Saturn V—slice through the atmosphere, then disappear into the heavens. With its outsized and heavy cargo (consisting of one-tenth of the planned Stepping Stone space station), the SS-1 spaceship entered Earth's orbit and jettisoned its 150-foot long booster. Over the next five hours, it fulfilled its centripetal revolutions, then, with a fiery blast, slingshot its way out toward the moon.

Just shy of twenty hours later, the huge SS-1 cargo ship entered the moon's orbit. The vessel had traveled 238,900 miles, and at a speed three-times faster than the Apollo missions. Each astronaut peered out of one of the capsule's four round portholes with anticipation as they gazed down at the heavily-pocked lunar surface: Sheila, eager to take soil samples; Eddie, to begin unloading and assembling the first section of the S^3's foundation; Bobby, to direct and partake in the assembly of his envisioned space station; while Commander Zimmer piloted the craft toward the landing site. However, as the ship descended, the klaxon blared! Simultaneously, all of the ship's computer screens flashed, *"Error! Error!"*

The ship's interior lights flickered, while the computer screens fractured with random pixels, when suddenly, everything blacked out!

"What the hell is going on?" Eddie panicked, while Sheila grasped Bobby's wrist and gazed into his eyes for reassurance.

Blake squinted as he pressed the power button several times to reboot, yet to no avail. As streams of sunlight pierced through the four windows, offering moderate visibility, Commander Zimmer crowed, "Blake, switch me to manual!"

"Affirmative!" Bobby responded.

Meanwhile, Zimmer swiftly gained control as the 500-foot cargo ship rattled and creaked under immense stress.

"We're coming in fast," Zimmer said, *"way* too fast!" he added, his voice marred with concern—so much so that the crew all gazed anxiously at him, while he wrestled with the vibrating controls.

Zimmer had always handled such glitches in the simulator with ease, but being in lunar orbit—with the moon's surface zooming toward him at several thousand miles per hour—made him feel like a kamikaze pilot on a suicide mission.

"What the hell is with this tin barge of yours, Blake?" Eddie screeched as he held on firmly to his armrest. "I knew the boy wonder would screw up, *somehow!*"

Sheila rolled her eyes and barked, "Not helpful, Eddie!"

Blake reached over and flicked a switch, which enabled an auxiliary unit to fire retro rockets. Their sudden and short-lived bursts jolted the ship and deadened their velocity, yet the auxiliary unit also flickered and went dead.

As the ship slowed to a manageable speed, Zimmer sighed. "Thanks, Blake! I think I got this space-tanker under control now. But for God's sake, where the hell are we? We've flown well past our intended trajectory, and all of our navigational computers are down. I'm flying blind."

"I'm sorry, I can't help you there, Commander," Bobby replied. "I'm still baffled as to what caused the malfunction. But I suggest we land, soon!"

Zimmer peered back at Blake. "Why soon? Is there something else that's wrong?"

"Well, y-yes, Commander," Bobby said, as his voice cracked with disappointment. "We're heading toward the dark side of the moon, which I'd prefer we avoid...at all costs."

Eddie's head snapped in Blake's direction. "Why is that?" he interrupted.

Prior to joining the team, Eddie had been a small-time

mechanic in Mobile, Alabama, and hadn't received much experience or training in astronomy or physics, a pet peeve of Commander Zimmer's, who had balked at his superiors about their selection. Yet, nepotism and an agenda to incorporate civilians into the program outweighed Zimmer's logical concerns.

"Oh, yeah!" Eddie reminded himself. "The dark side never gets any sunlight."

Bobby gazed over at Eddie. "No, Eddie, that's a fallacy. Both sides of the moon experience two weeks of sunlight each month. It's just that the dark side always faces *away* from Earth. So even if we regain power, we'll be—"

Before he finished, Zimmer had no choice but to land several miles into the dark side, as the ship touched ground with a hard *bang* and ominous *thud.*

"Shit!" Eddie barked, as he glared at Blake. "We'll be *what*, Bobby?"

Blake's head dropped. "Well, basically… We'll be… I guess the word is marooned—our radio signals won't be able to reach Earth."

Eddie unbuckled himself and drifted upward. "Jesus Christ! Are you fuckin' kidding me?" He cocked his head sideways as he grabbed on to a metal buttress to stabilize himself. "You *guess* the word is marooned? You mean fucked! Right? As in majorly fucked!"

"Calm down!" Zimmer commanded.

Sheila added, "He's right, Eddie. Enough of the testosterone! That's *not* helpful. How about we all *use* our heads, rather than *lose* our heads?"

Eddie shot Sheila a Taser-like stare, one that could almost short circuit the ship a second time.

Meanwhile, Bobby stood up and, without a word, inspected their space suits, to ensure they had power.

Fortunately, they did, as their battery packs had been well insulated. He then turned and quietly began investigating the ship's electronic systems.

Eddie's face reddened with animus. He couldn't get over how Blake had ignored him. He clenched his fists and made a move to confront him, when Zimmer astutely commanded, "Eddie and Sheila, gear up and examine the exterior of the ship for damages. Then explore the surrounding terrain. Do it. Now!"

With a grunt, Eddie gritted his teeth and complied, while Sheila rolled her eyes. She didn't know why she kept getting saddled with her ornery team member, but decided that once they left the ship, she'd wander off and take soil samples, believing that moon rocks might have more intelligence than the rocks in Eddie's head.

Some forty minutes or so after they exited the ship, Zimmer finally turned toward Blake. "I need the ugly truth, Blake. How bad is it?"

Bobby had already inspected most of the main computer and electric board, and now briefly pulled his head out of the access panel. "It's not good, Commander." He turned and stuck his head back into the main computer's chassis.

"Bobby!" Zimmer barked.

Startled, Bobby bumped his head as he backed out. Rubbing his bruise, he gazed at the commander. "Yes, sir?"

"Extrapolate, please!"

Blake shook his head, disappointed. "At present, it's an enigma, sir. There's nothing I can see in my design that could blow out all of our electronic equipment like this." As he verbalized those thoughts, it suddenly struck him. "Unless, of course, it had nothing at all to do with my hardware or software. It could have been by a solar flare."

His eyes lit up. "Correction—something *this* powerful must have been a CME."

Zimmer squinted, then twisted his lips. "Okay, Professor Egghead. In English, please?"

Blake shrugged. "Sorry, sir. CME stands for Coronal Mass Ejection. It's somewhat akin to a solar flare, but far more powerful and disruptive. Its electromagnetic waves have been known to last for several hours, and have blown out entire electrical grids on Earth. In fact, the first recorded solar storm dates all the way back to 1859, when the then new telegraph system was zapped dead. Many telegraphers even received severe electric shocks."

Zimmer's face turned pale. "Are you saying our systems have been irreparably damaged... By the *sun*?"

"I don't wish to be a pessimist, sir, but currently, I believe so."

"Currently?" Zimmer pressed.

Bobby forced out a half-smile through his nervous lips. "Well, like I said, sir. I hate to be a pessimist. So, there must be a workaround, somehow."

As Zimmer smiled, Bobby scratched his head again and said, "Well, correction. Not *must* be. More like, *might* be a workaround. I just need more time to think this through."

Zimmer nodded. "Yes, you do that. That's why I sent those two out to reconnoiter the area. Not that I expect any moon creatures to be plotting an attack, but my military experience knows when to keep idle minds busy and distracted from depression, or, God forbid, from committing violent acts borne out of fear. Unless, that is, you need them to assist you in any way?"

Blake had been sitting in almost a trance while Zimmer rambled on, but then the commander reached over and tapped Bobby's knee. "You still with me?" As Bobby jerked and looked at him, Zimmer added, "I hope you're not wigging out on me, are you?"

Bobby quasi-smiled. "Hell no, sir. I've just been thinking." He spun around and gazed out the capsule window. "Just over that dark horizon there's not only sunlight, but also a direct view—and line of communication—with good ol' Mother Earth."

Zimmer squinted. "But that must be a several-hours-long hike from here. And Eddie and Sheila have used up a good hour of their two-hour oxygen tanks already. That only leaves two more full tanks, with two hours of oxygen each—yours and mine."

"Yes," Bobby said. "So, I will need to take yours with me."

"What the hell are you saying, Blake? You're the mastermind here, the father of all this equipment. I can't afford to lose you on such a dangerous mission. That might only be enough oxygen to get you there. It's suicide."

"Commander, yes, the trek to the lit side of the moon is probably two to four hours away, but if it's more than that, the mission will fail. And being a marathon runner and the youngest person here with the best physical stats, I'm the only logical choice. I'm well trained to conserve oxygen while also having the stamina to make long distance runs."

Zimmer's face turned indignant. "I won't have it, Blake! You're indispensable. For God's sake, I'd much prefer sending Eddie out there. Yes, he's a mechanic, but so are you, only a helluva lot smarter and an astroengineer. And your brain is desperately required in this grim situation. Christ, as you said earlier, we're marooned, unless you can do whatever it is you're scheming to do. And come to think of it—what *are* you thinking of doing?"

Blake started to gather his gear. "As I said, our electronic system has been short-circuited by a CME. In essence, it's fried. However, I kept several high voltage batteries, shortwave walkie-talkies, and a high-powered portable transmitter inside this lead-lined compartment." As he pulled them out and stuffed them into his left and right side-packs, he continued, "So, they have not been damaged by solar radiation. Once I reach the sunlit side of the moon, I'll also have a direct view and line of communication with Earth."

"So basically, you'll phone home, like ET." Zimmer said with a smile of admiration, one that quickly faded. "But damn it, Blake, you're the youngest one on board." His voice mellowed. "And a newlywed, for God's sake. I truly have deep reservations about this, Blake. And if you don't make it, well—we're all dead."

Bobby put his helmet on and locked it. "Well, we'll all *positively* be dead if I *don't* go, Commander. That's indisputable." Unexpectedly, somber thoughts about Suzy flooded his mind. Blake choked up as he tried to suppress the painful memories and tears that were rapidly mounting. "Either way, I won't ever s-see my wife again, sir, which I hate to even t-think about." His voice cracked. "But I can at least save all of *you*, and hopefully my dream. If this mission is a total disaster, NASA will scrap it and mankind will linger in a malaise for another fifty years. I can't and *won't* allow that to happen."

Regaining his bearing, he continued, "So, this is not foolish bravado, sir. It's pure statistics: none of you could run as fast, or as far, as I can to catch sight of Earth, without wasting oxygen and jeopardizing this life-and-death mission. If the trek requires more than four hours of oxygen, well then—" he nervously paused. "We're all doomed."

Quickly regaining his vigor, he went on, "But you know darn well, sir, that I'm the favorite racehorse to bet on if it requires less."

Zimmer cracked a smile, appreciating Blake's shrewd use of an equestrian analogy, knowing his penchant for horse racing, as Blake added, "Granted, we have no way of knowing exactly how far away this destination is, but if it *is* less, I'm your Seabiscuit, and I *guarantee* I'll make it."

Zimmer had to chuckle internally at Blake's colorful pitch and youthful optimism, but once again he smirked. "I hate to break the news to you, Bobby, but...there are *no* guarantees in life."

Blake nodded solemnly. "That might be true, Colonel. Believe me, if there was another option, I would gladly consider it. But the clock is ticking, and we're losing precious time."

With that, Bobby Blake handed Colonel Zimmer a shortwave walkie-talkie and entered the air lock. He checked all his equipment, took a deep breath, and then stepped out onto the dark side of the moon.

Bobby reached for the control pad on his left forearm and turned on his helmet's spotlight. A narrow, funnel-shaped beam lit up before him, yet its paltry luminance faded to black less than 20 yards away, easily swallowed up by the eerie darkness. All around him was pitch black, as the lunar surface melded with the heavens and engulfed him, like a death shroud. Only tiny specks of stars glittered, along with a glimmer of sunlight on the horizon that formed a faint lunar corona.

Blake adjusted the two oxygen tanks on his back and started sprinting with an awkward stride, hindered by the moon's limited gravity. As he took long, aerial leaps, he felt like a cosmic ballerina, or better yet, he thought, like a flying warrior in *Crouching Tiger, Hidden Dragon.*

†††

Forty minutes after Blake's departure, Sheila and Eddie finally returned to the ship, only to be confronted by Commander Zimmer, who relayed Blake's daring mission.

Nervously, Sheila slowly took off her suit, not thrilled with the latest news. Meanwhile, Eddie's hopes skyrocketed. He grasped the walkie-talkie and clicked the button. "Hey, Bobby-boy! I knew I could count on you. Fly like the wind, Icarus!"

Blake rolled his eyes. He wasn't sure if Eddie had no idea who Icarus was, or if he'd intentionally jabbed him with a sardonic needle. But he knew as sure as hell he didn't want to be like Icarus. He shook his head and ignored the Greek tragedy as he replied, "Roger that, Eddie. But don't drain the batteries. If I don't succeed, you'll have to devise another plan, and those batteries might be your only key to survival. For your information, I used the remaining high-powered batteries to run the auxiliary units there, but they likewise must be used sparingly. You only have about four days of power, that's it. Over and out."

Eddie's mind, however, was currently fixated on one thing only: how Bobby ignored his witty mythological compliment, like he had ignored him earlier. Eddie's face twisted into a snarl, as his ten fingers clenched into two fists. But then, a frightening thought obliterated his petty grievance.

Eddie turned toward Zimmer. "Hey, Commander! Only *four days* of power! Is he kidding me? Once those batteries die, so too will our HVAC system. Then we'll freeze, like frozen sardines in this shitty little can! We'll all be dead!"

Nonchalantly, Zimmer continued writing in his personal diary without even making eye contact. "That's *why* he's making a precarious trek, Eddie. I already explained that."

"Yeah, you explained *his* mission," Eddie snapped, "but not *our* limited power here on the ship." Eddie's frazzled mechanical mind rumbled like a crankcase without oil, as he added, "And just what *are* the odds, anyhow? I mean, of him succeeding, or rather—us dying?"

Zimmer calmly turned and gazed—not at Eddie—but out of the porthole, spotting the pinhead-sized shimmer of Blake's headlamp in the far distance. "I guess about fifty-fifty, Eddie." Zimmer suddenly imagined the moving speck of light to be a thoroughbred, as he added, "But despite all my years of betting, the odds have always been in the track's favor. So, I'm no expert, Eddie, by any means. But I pray to God we have a Man O' War out there."

Eddie squinted, not realizing Man O' War was actually a horse, as Zimmer turned and looked hard and deep into Eddie's eyes. "And for your information, Plato, Icarus attempted to fly to the sun, but his wings caught fire and he plunged to his death. So, spare us any further bad omens, will you?"

†††

Meanwhile, Bobby had been racing along, like Secretariat with weighted moon boots, while his heart, lungs, and legs all pumped in sync. Yet, out of the darkness, a huge ridge emerged! As the crest rapidly approached, Blake tried to stop, but lunar inertia kept his body moving, as he literally flew over the edge. It was too late—Bobby now realized he was airborne and headed right into a huge crater. His body tumbled down the steep incline, while lunar dust billowed in his wake. It was several moments later when he finally rolled to a dead stop. Lying on his back, his helmet's spotlight illuminated the fine dust as it passed over him, engulfing him in a nebulous mist.

"Shit!" he cussed. As he lay there, he thought about all the training he had back on Earth in weightless chambers. Oddly enough, those exercises never allowed him to understand the true buoyancy and speed he now acquired by running on the moon. Blake frowned. He now realized his mobility had to be managed with greater awareness of the advancing terrain.

Awkwardly, he rolled to his side in his cumbersome spacesuit, laden with gear, then stood up and inspected it and all his equipment. He was relieved that his headlamp was not damaged. His head swiveled, like a lighthouse in the night, as he gazed at the eerie void, then up at the jet-black sky. It was speckled with distant stars, planets, and fanciful constellations; a cosmos that has enamored mankind for countless millennia.

He blinked hard and thanked the Almighty Force of the Universe for allowing him to survive the fall unscathed. He had long given up on the Judeo-Christian God and all the numerous others worshipped on Earth, with their hypocritical, illogical, or spiteful ways, but knew that, far beyond mankind's limited capacity, a Supreme Entity of some type had to have created this vast and miraculous symphony of stars and planets, which precisely floated, rotated, and revolved in an unfathomably immense vacuum. And being out in space only amplified Blake's feeling of insignificance and reverence for something far greater than anything allegedly known—or conjured up—by mankind.

Once again, Bobby pointed his body in the direction of the distant glimmer of sunlight and started to run, hop, and fly as fast (but as cautiously) as he could. The fleeting minutes turned into well over an hour, as his heart beat faster and sweat moistened the inside of his suit.

Frightful thoughts of the studies of how the human mind cracks amid darkness for long spells filled his head. As he dashed through the black and barren lunar landscape, he was beginning to become unnerved, when suddenly, warm thoughts of Suzy materialized out of the chilling void. This time, they weren't longings marred with dread, but were blissful memories of the deep love they shared, which acted like white blood cells to ward off infectious thoughts, whereby suppressing the fear and depression that threatened to invade his mind and devour his will. Visions of their first date, their first kiss, numerous adventures, and laughs lifted his heart and gave it the stamina to go on.

With a deep breath, a wave of confidence came over him, as his mind stipulated: *I will succeed, and I will return to the ship! And, by God, I will see my beloved once again. This will all become just a bad dream — a nightmare, rather — that will only arise during my recollections, when we'll both laugh at this specter of death while we sip our champagne and watch TV in a loving embrace.*

Blake was reenergized, and now had every intention of making his mission a success, for everyone. With both ventricles jettisoning blood like a Johnny pump, Bobby's legs propelled his body across the huge crater's dreary valley. The minutes flew by, as Blake kept his mind in the zone, just like he had during his many marathons. Periodically, he peered down at his forearm's control panel, keeping a watchful eye on his vitals, while his mind read the data: *heart rate, fine; blood pressure, fine; lung oxygenation, fine. My spirits, super fine! I can do this.*

His eyes veered from the vitals gauges to the bouncing spotlight beam before him, which still vaguely lit the lunar surface. Beyond that, he could see the lunar corona becoming somewhat brighter—he had made good progress. However, several minutes later, Blake's stride took a downturn and he felt lightheaded.

He glanced down at his oxygen gauge: the first tank was seconds away from empty. Bobby slowed to a stop and took a deep breath, sucking in the last molecules of oxygen out of the tank. He then held his breath, detached the tank, and tossed it to the ground. Yet as he activated the spare tank, a grim thought crept into his head. Suddenly, his heart sank and his hands trembled. He had hoped he would have reached sight of Earth with one tank, but he had now reached the moment he most dreaded: *the point of no return.*

He gazed back in the direction of the spaceship. His throat tightened with anxiety. The horrifying time had arrived: he now knew he had only two hours left to live— 120 minutes, or just 7,200 seconds. Yet, what *if* he turned back?

His head rotated toward the moon's corona of sunlight, then back toward the ship. He was at the ultimate crossroad in his life. He realistically calculated the probability of successfully returning to the ship to be forty-seven percent. But, he also knew that humans have a propensity to ignore deadly facts and beat the odds—akin to how they know they can't avoid death, yet they block it from their minds and move onward, many times surpassing ages they had erroneously consigned themselves to.

Bobby knew he had to do the same: block death out of his mind. Not for his own sake—since he now realized, there *were* guarantees in life: namely, he *would* be dead in 7,102 seconds—but rather for the sake of his crew, who all had a chance to survive, *if* he succeeded. His eyes oscillated to the disturbing thoughts in his head. To return to the ship now would guarantee only one thing: all of their deaths. That, he now knew, was indisputable. It was also something he had no control over. Hence, harsh reality stared Blake in the face. The Grim Reaper awaited him in either direction. Yet, what he would do with those remaining seconds in his life was something he *did* have control over.

He unzipped the small breast pocket on his spacesuit and pulled out a photo of Suzy. Tenderly, he rubbed the photo with his thick glove, yet was annoyed he couldn't kiss it. He wanted desperately to feel it with his lips—to feel at least a sense of her. He pressed the photo against his faceplate and, with an aching heart, kissed the air, knowing this was the closest he would ever get to his beloved. There would be no happy reunion. There would be no looking back to laugh at this specter of death, for death had already won the macabre game. This was the end.

Bobby slipped the photo back inside his pocket and swallowed hard. He adjusted his gear, turned toward the distant sunlight, and started to run once again. Yet, after several steps, his leg buckled with intense pain, causing him to fall to his knees. He grabbed his calf and began massaging the ache as he rose to his feet. His mind reeled. *What the hell is this? I'm a marathon runner, for God's sake. I don't get severe cramps this easily.*

Bobby turned and looked down the length of his back. His eyes bulged! A pebble-sized meteorite had blown through his oxygen tank and smashed into the back of his leg. Quickly, he looked at his gauge: one of the two inner chambers was losing air, rapidly!

He felt his stomach turn as a tear began to form in his eye. "Shit! No, no, no! This can't be. It just can't be!"

Not realizing the button on his walkie-talkie had been depressed, Zimmer's voice rang out, "What is it, Blake? Are you all right?"

Bobby released the button and closed his eyes to regain a sense of calm, then responded, "Yes, sir. Just a minor glitch. Maintain radio silence until I reach sight of Earth. Over and out."

He bit his lip. It was now imperative: he had to pick up the pace, *somehow*. But as he stepped forward, the ache in his calf shot painful needles up his leg, almost causing him to fall again. Blake knew the warning signs; he surely had ligament damage and internal bleeding from the missile-like impact of the meteorite. His trek would be severely hindered, if not a failure already.

A wave of anguish threatened to malign his will, yet Blake took a deep breath and exhaled slowly. He realized his good fortune: namely, that the meteorite had hit the metal tank first. Otherwise, it would have blown straight through his suit and leg, while the minus 455-degree frigid, lunar temperature would have rendered him dead in seconds.

He gazed back up to the black heavens. *I guess I should thank you, not curse you. Whoever you are. But it would have been nice if you allowed me to run.*

With a heavy sigh, Blake resumed his quest as he limped along and gazed down at his digital clock, watching the few seconds remaining of his life tick away: *click, tick, click, tick...*

With only 6,003 seconds left to live, the countdown seemed to go faster as he struggled with each annoying limp and painful hobble. He decided, for his sanity, it was best to not even look at the clock, yet the pain in his calf only increased with each step. He hopped on one foot, trying to alleviate the pain, but he found that the awkward stride and slow pace only frustrated him more. He stopped a moment and massaged his leg, when, out of the corner of his eye, he saw a faint reflection. Or at least he thought it was a reflection.

He stood upright, turned slightly, then peered through the dark abyss of the crater's huge valley, when his eyes spotted something. It was definitely *something*, but something not of the moon, but rather something quite miraculous. He blinked hard to make sure it wasn't a mirage. And, as sure as his love for Suzy, the beautiful vision before him was an Earthly delight: a true miracle!

He hopped as fast as he could and finally came upon the glorious apparition. There before him was the defunct Soviet lunar rover, *Lunokhod 2*.

A huge grin lit up Bobby's face. "Wow! You beautiful old buggy—you're the world record holder for most miles driven on an alien surface." Affectionately, he ran his gloved hand over its metallic skin. "Well, that is, until NASA's Mars Opportunity rover beat you. But that's okay, that's okay, L2. I'm so glad to see you!" His eyes scanned and savored every inch of the odd-looking vehicle. His emotions were getting the better of him, for just to see something man-made in the lunar void brought a tear to his eye. "You truly are a sight for sore eyes."

But can I get you to run again?

Blake's photographic memory about the Soviet robotic rover came flashing back: specifically, how its eight, metal-grated wheels, with sharp, fin-like treads, were each independently powered by electric motors. And despite its very slow speed, Bobby quickly figured that the high-voltage battery in his utility-pack would be powerful enough to make the two front wheels propel the vehicle to thirty miles an hour, at least for a limited time, until the battery ran dead or the motors burnt out.

Elated, Blake set to work on retrofitting the lunar vehicle.

†††

Meanwhile, back at the SS-1 spaceship, Eddie had suited up and discreetly exited the capsule's helm, while Zimmer and Sheila continued their diagnostics. As Zimmer was fiddling with a control panel, he heard the airlock. He spun around and dashed to a portal window, only to see Eddie walk to and enter the rear cargo section of the huge craft.

Zimmer smirked. "Of course, the cargo section has more oxygen than our capsule. The sneaky bastard!"

Sheila unstrapped herself from her seat. "Should I suit up and go back there, Commander?"

Zimmer huffed. "No. I knew he was a bad fit from the start, but the mighty directors—who sit up in their big, flashy offices—always know better than those on the ground. Or so they think. Not that his being a cousin of Director Morgan's had anything to do with it." He gazed at Sheila and shook his head. "Let the scared, little lab rat suck up all the oxygen back there, he only left more for us up here. And frankly, everything bears upon Blake's mission, as all the oxygen in the world is useless if an SOS is not sent to Earth."

No sooner did those words emanate from his mouth than a ripping explosion rocked the ship. Zimmer and Sheila collided into each other and then floated into adjacent walls, bouncing off of instrument panels.

With the ship in a blackout, they had no way of knowing how bad the damage was until they peered out the portals. Their eyes widened as they saw the rear cargo section of the ship blasted apart, the fuselage's skin ripped and torn like aluminum foil.

It was clear: Eddie was dead.

Both of their faces washed white with shock as they each regretted their harsh words toward their fellow, and now fallen, astronaut. Yet, as the capsule still vibrated from the aftershock, their minds quickly veered to another tract; namely, self-preservation.

Dear God, how bad is the damage? Zimmer thought.

While Sheila fretted, *Were the capsule's oxygen tanks compromised?*

The next thought, however, was apparent to both of them: one of them would have to go out and examine the wreckage.

Zimmer volunteered. "There's only one tank left, and it only has twenty minutes of oxygen in it. I'll go."

Sheila grabbed her suit. "Commander, that's *my* tank!" she said forcefully. "So back off. Spare me the macho crap. *I'll* go."

Zimmer shook his head with admiration as he watched her suit up. "Very well. But here's the trade-off. Take the walkie-talkie. If our capsule's oxygen tank was damaged, you can radio Blake the dismal news. Because his mission will be useless, and you'll return here to a corpse. I won't wait for my last breath of air from this metal tomb, Sheila. *I'll* dictate my exit, not some measly molecule of oxygen."

Zimmer gave her a solemn hug, as tears welled in her eyes.

"Let's hope for t-the best, s-shall we?" Sheila uttered, nervously.

The seventeen minutes Shelia was gone seemed like an eternity to Zimmer, until she returned, thankfully with good news, at least for them. Their capsule and its oxygen tank were spared from being critically damaged. However,

Shelia choked up when she relayed that she had found several pieces of Eddie's remains, all charred and strewn among the rubble. They decided it was best to not mention the tragedy to Blake. He had enough of a burden on his shoulders, perhaps the greatest burden anyone could ever carry.

†††

Back out in the lunar void, Bobby had finished retrofitting the *Lunokhod 2*. He stood back and admired the machine and his good fortune. Then he leaned forward and smacked the top of the vehicle for good luck, ironically on its dead solar cells. Realizing his *faux pas*, he bent over and smacked the wheel instead. He was about to power up the wheels, when he noticed two Soviet plaques attached to the rover: one was the USSR emblem, the other, an engraving of Vladimir Lenin.

Blake smirked. "Seriously? *You*, of all people, a representative of Earth? I don't think so!"

He detached the Lenin plaque, placed it under the metal-grated front wheel, then hopped on the rover and powered it up. With a jolt, the *Lunokhod 2* sprung back to life, as its four sharp metal wheels sliced, chopped, and crushed Lenin's metallic face.

Blake smiled while he held on tight to the domed vehicle as it lurched and hummed its way forward. As it sped over the pockmarked valley of the lunar crater, creating a trail of dust in its wake, an old memory seeped into his head: the Russians actually no longer owned the celebrated L2. American video game developer and astronaut, Richard Garriott, had bought the rover, along with the *Luna 21* lander, for $68,500 in 1993 from the Russians, and became the only private citizen to own something tangible on the moon's surface.

Blake chuckled. *Sorry, Richard, that's what you get for leaving your vehicle unattended.*

As the motors screamed with high voltage and the wheels chewed up the lunar soil, Blake could see the sunlight ahead as it approached more rapidly. Although he couldn't *feel* the warmth of the sun through his regulated suit, the warm ambience of the sun's light lifted his spirits as the frigid darkness of night faded behind him. Before him, the gray lunar terrain was all aglow, while its myriad of dimpled craters cast deep shadows across the alien landscape.

Blake was full of anticipation, for the ultimate moment of euphoria was yet to come, as the glorious vision of Earth finally appeared on the horizon. His heart lifted as his eyes saw the Earth's beautiful blue and white crest peek over the barren summits of the lunar mountains.

Just then, the rover's over-heated electric motors and battery burned out as the *Lunokhod 2* coasted some eighty yards and came to a stop. Blake stood up on the dome of the rover and anxiously pulled out his transmitter, which he plugged into his suit's audio system. Nervously, he fumbled with the unit, located the power button, and eagerly pressed it.

Nothing?

Again, he pressed the button, this time harder.

But again, *nothing!*

He gazed up at the heavens and cried, "No! You can't do this to me! It's not fair!"

Quickly, he removed the transmitter's rear panel, then disconnected and reconnected the battery, with the hopes that it was just a bad connection. He pressed the button again and again, yet to no avail. He shook his head vehemently as he peered back up at the glorious Earth within his view. *No! No! No! This can't be!*

Bobby's stomach twisted into an ugly knot as he fell back. As he sat on top of the rover, tears broke free and coursed down his cheeks. Crestfallen, he pulled out the battery once again and inspected it closer. He was baffled; there was nothing visibly wrong with it. Nevertheless, it was *dead*, just like the mission, and just like he would be in a matter of minutes. He punched his helmet. It was all for naught. He failed.

His mind went dark. *There are indeed* no *guarantees in life, except that we all die in the end!*

He gritted his teeth, and with a primal grunt, threw the battery. It flew for several yards into the distance, then landed and slid to a stop. His head fell as a maelstrom of malignant thoughts besieged him.

Bobby gazed angrily at the useless transmitter in his hand, and wanted to throw it, too, when suddenly, it blinked and vibrated! Its screen lit up and the power-indicator bar extended across the screen and registered 100 percent.

Blake squinted. *What the... This can't be.*

Yet, the strange unit continued to defy all logic and physics as it glowed and hummed to life. He looked up at the heavens. *Dear Lord, yes! Oh, yes, yes, yes! It can be. Thank you! Thank you, sweet Lord. It's a miracle!* Baffled, Blake gazed down at the transmitter and pushed the proper buttons, which all seemed to function perfectly. *But how could they? I don't get it!* his mind reeled.

Then it happened: a voice rang out of the transmitter!

"SS-1, come in. Are you there, SS-1? Come in, *please*, SS-1. Do you read me?"

Blake eagerly pressed the button. *"Yes!* Yes! I read you!" he replied. "Loud and clear, Houston! This is Blake. Bobby Blake."

As the sun reflected off the transmitter's chrome frame, it suddenly dawned on him: CME solar storms have been known to power electric equipment with their intense magnetic radiation levels, which often last several hours. He glanced up at the bright yellow orb and winked. The *miracle* had a scientific explanation, after all.

"Mayday! Mayday!" he cried into the transmitter. "Ship damaged by CME. Sitting approximately twenty miles away from the Le Monnier crater at 25.85 degrees north, 30.45 degrees east. Home of *Lunokhod 2.* How soon can you assemble a rescue team?"

Bobby smiled to himself. His photographic memory remembered the exact coordinates of the defunct Soviet rover from his days of studying it in college. Excitedly, he simultaneously radioed Zimmer on the walkie-talkie and relayed the good news, then disengaged when he heard Houston's glorious response.

"Blake, by God! We thought you all were…I mean, by God, so good to hear from you! Rescue flight will be readied for launch ASAP. Can you all hold out for seventy-two hours?"

The joyful taste of success in Bobby's mouth turned sour as reality hit him, once again, like a cheap punch to the solar plexus. His glorious grin mellowed to a somber stiff upper lip. "Well, *the crew* is there, Houston. As for *me,* well— I journeyed out of the dark side, some thirty miles or more, into visual range to communicate, Houston. And, well, I'm just about out of oxygen." With a painful crack in his voice, he murmured, "C-Can you p-please tell… my wife that—"

"Hold on, Blake. Your wife is right here, worried sick. I mean, oh Jesus. Well, she's right here. Hold on."

Bobby swallowed hard as a meaty lump constricted his throat.

Then he heard it: the soft and beautiful voice of his beloved, the soul mate he had plans of sharing the rest of his life with. The woman who, unbeknownst to all, had recently learned that she was pregnant. The thought of never getting to see his son or daughter was like a vise clamped on his heart, and each word she spoke was like another painful twist, crushing his heart into pulp.

"Oh, Bobby, m-my love. Why, oh w-why?"

Blake heard the strain in her voice and closed his eyes; the pain was too much to bear, for both of them.

"Say no more, my love. I know. I know. Lord knows, I love you...beyond the stars, beyond the very universe itself," he said as he glanced out into the infinite blackness of space. "Hopefully we will meet again one day, sweetheart. Somewhere. Somewhere out *here* in this silent symphony of eternal mystery."

As he gazed back at Earth—which floated peacefully in eerie silence amid a black void speckled with twinkling stars—Blake once again felt the humble insignificance of mankind and the grandeur of an endless and complex universe, far beyond the microscopic grasp of the human mind. Solemnly, he bowed his head in reverence while tears streamed down his youthful face.

Unable to wipe away the tears, he blinked hard to clear his eyes, then pulled out his cherished photograph of Suzy and gazed at it. "I'm so sorry I couldn't make it back home, Suzy." He paused, as the lump in his throat seemed to grow, like a tumor; a cancerous, evil knot that he knew would soon consume and steal his life, ripping him away from everything he loved.

He pressed the photo tight against his heart and swallowed hard. "Please, you must find another... M-man who will love our child as his own, and love and c-care for y-you... For the r-rest of your days," he stammered. It was the most painful sentence he'd ever had to utter, one he never dreamed he would ever have need to, as his hand clenched the transmitter tighter, struggling to harness his emotions. The pain of knowing he'd never get the chance to share the joyous life he envisioned with her ripped through him like a chainsaw.

All the grand adventures of traveling the world together were now gone. The Mars mission milestones he hoped to achieve, with her lovingly at his side as his muse, gone. All the passionate nights of sublime ecstasy, uniting as one, gone. And even the monumental joys of fatherhood had now been stolen from him, gone.

The malignant lump in his throat grew larger and tighter, latching its tentacles around his vocal cords and choking his words. "I... I w-wish I could b-be with you, Suzy, but... This d-dark day *will* pass.... I must b-become a m-memory, not a mooring. Do you hear me? You m-must set sail and seize the brighter days ahead of you...and make a healthy l-loving home for our b-beautiful child. Promise me, Suzy... *don't die with me.*" He struggled to breathe. "You m-must go on... and live... *Live for me.*"

Suzy's tearful voice confirmed her promise, as Blake gasped for air. He glanced down at his oxygen gauge: it displayed the dreaded word *"Empty.".* It was too soon; he wanted more time. Tears saturated his face as he kept the precious photo pressed to his aching heart. He peered back up at Earth, took his last look, and blew a kiss with his final breath, as his lungs convulsed and heart buckled with a dying spasm.

Blake's life, and the pain, were gone.

Blake's dead body teetered momentarily in weightlessness, then fell—almost as if in slow motion— landing on the dome of the dead *L2* rover amid a dead terrain of dry dust.

Meanwhile, the gut-wrenching whimpers of his beloved Suzy emanated from the speaker, until the solar radiation dissipated and died, along with her laments and the transmitter—returning the lunar surface to its eerie, but normal, state of dead silence.

†††

Back at the ship, Zimmer and Sheila sat mute, overwhelmed by the tragic, yet miraculous, denouement. Death had spawned life. Blake's heroic sacrifice had given life to not only his compatriots but also to his dream, which Zimmer and Sheila vowed to make sure NASA would fulfill.

Undying gratitude mixed with sorrow welled in their breasts as they pensively gazed up at the stars and waited for the rescue team; no longer plagued by fear and death, and—with eternal thanks to Bobby Blake—no longer marooned on the dark side of the moon.

SLUMBER MOUNTAIN

Freydis pushed her way through the throng of Vikings—most of low standing, bearing beat-up axes, while several noblemen sported finely-crafted Carolingian swords—and stood before her famous brother, the Chieftain of Greenland.

Leif Erikson smirked at his spirited sister, with her magnetic green eyes and long red hair tied into two braids, and awaited her charge, one he was becoming more accustomed to hearing over the past year.

Freydis's lips twisted as she crossed her muscular arms. "So, when will you grant us our leave, dear brother? I'm tired of Greenland, and tired of waiting!" She glanced at the stout gang of Vikings around her. "As are these fine men. And forget about the old world, Leif. We all know you found a *New World* two years ago, and even built a cabin there. Yet you abandoned it. I, for one, would like to go to this place, which you called Vinland, and make a permanent settlement."

Leif huffed. He was used to her pleas to live elsewhere—be it the familiar lands of their Scandinavian neighbors, or even the cities of mainland Europe that their ancestors had sacked—but her new destination into the uncharted New World was another matter.

"Freydis! I abandoned it because the natives there are hostile. The Skraeling are *not* to be trusted. Furthermore, my mission of Christianizing Greenland has taken precedence. Therefore, I strongly suggest that—"

"If you lost your nerve, brother," Freydis cut in with a sarcastic bite, "then give *me* a damn crew! *I'll* show you how to make a permanent settlement!"

As several Vikings chuckled, Leif's irritated face couldn't conceal his frustration. He'd been sick of his sister badgering him since his return last year in 1009 AD, and now her crass insult—in front of many of his loyal men, no less—was too much. If she were a man he would have throttled her, but instead he took a deep breath as he glanced at the large assemblage of Norsemen.

Leif was torn: despite her feisty bite, he knew that his obstinate sister had a point; many of his men—including Thorfinn Karlsefni and his new wife, Gudrid, who happened to be Leif's former sister-in-law—had grown restless, as had many local villagers. While some merely sought adventure, others were in dire need of carving out a living, or longed to settle down and start families. How could he deny them? Sure, Greenland was nice—the land that, in fact, his father, Erik the Red, first settled—but nature often instilled in the human heart a longing that the grass is greener on the other side. That's even why his father named Greenland as such, to entice followers to settle on the *greener* landmass *on the other side* of the then-known world, despite the fact that much of Greenland was an icy glacier.

But the restless nature of mankind often made contentment fleeting, and the undiscovered world to the west might just offer such a place. Yet, the land Leif had labeled Vinland may have been rich with grapes to make wine, but it was not as hospitable as he had hoped. Leif glanced at the large gathering of familiar faces before him as he scratched his wiry beard. His grave reservations gave way to another thought: just because *he* had become weary of such endeavors and gave up—in order to follow his evangelical mission at home—didn't mean he should quash the yearnings of others. Moreover, his strong-willed sister had a burning flame within her breast that couldn't be easily snuffed much longer.

Leif gazed at his sister and shook his head in submission. "Very well, Freydis." He looked over at Thorfinn, then at the throng of Viking men and several women, and said, "If any of you wish to take this long and precarious journey, then by all means, do so. Thorfinn…" He glanced at Freydis, "along with my sister, will guide you. May the Lord, Jesus Christ, watch over you."

While most Vikings erupted with cheers, others rolled their eyes at the Christian who abandoned not only Vinland, but also their pagan Norse Gods. The majority of Vikings still had the savage blood of warriors within their bodies. As such, they longed for the honor of being lauded in Valhalla for gallantry in battle. The mere thought of meekly passing through St. Peter's Gate for having lived a humble life not only seemed ridiculous, but actually repulsed them. However, the crowd that gathered for this expedition had been of a more peaceful bent—even if somewhat crude—who longed for something better, whatever *better* might be. Nevertheless, they all eagerly gathered their gear and headed toward their respective longships.

Meanwhile, Leif glanced back at Freydis, and discreetly chided, "And if you ever embarrass me like that again, I'll strangle you with your own braids!"

Freydis smiled as she stroked her long, rusty pigtails and kissed him on the cheek. She whispered in his ear, "Just try it!" as she grabbed his balls. "And I'll crush these grapes like the ones you found on Vinland!"

Leif couldn't resist chuckling as he kissed her forehead and pushed her away. "Now get out of here, you crazy maiden, before I spank you!"

Freydis looked deep into his eyes. "Thank you, you won't regret it. Thorfinn and I will bring back rich tales of our journey and the new settlements that will expand our reach across the seas to distant worlds."

"Well, I gave you instructions how to find Vinland, but as I said, you'll need to make settlements elsewhere. Heed my warning, sis. And good luck."

Freydis nodded warmly. "Don't worry, if we run into any hostile bastards, we'll whip their stinking asses into shape, or cut off their mangy sacks."

As she started to walk away, Leif shook his head once again. "Just be careful. And for the love of God, try not to curse so much!"

†††

Three longships, each carrying forty passengers, set sail into the icy waters off the coast of Greenland. Three weeks later, with no hospitable land in sight, the clouds turned gray and blistering gales swept across the frigid waters. The ships tossed and pitched as they scaled the frothy crests of the North Atlantic and slammed down into its rolling valleys. Meanwhile, oarsmen fought to maintain control.

As seawater sprayed over the decks and weary crew, Thorfinn glanced at his men and winked—glad that he reminded them to apply beeswax and fish oil to their clothes to repel water. With his face and beard dripping, Thorfinn steered the lead ship through the swells. Right behind, Freydis followed, who suddenly took hold of the rudder, when the helmsman keeled over and vomited. With aplomb, Freydis navigated the ship between the mounting icebergs, some of which brushed up against the hull, making unnerving scraping sounds that further rattled the crew. Several Norsemen grabbed the railings and threw up, while others questioned their decision to leave the safety of home for *this*.

It was nearing dusk when one of the men bellowed with glee, "Land ho!"

With their rudders turned toward shore, the three longships made landfall, as the Viking crews eagerly secured their vessels amid the blistering winds. Wasting no time, Thorfinn instructed others to set up camp on the rocky beach.

Four hours later, the moon made its long-awaited appearance, as strong winds routed away the gray clouds and the night quelled into an eerie silence. Gazing up at the heavens, ninety-two Vikings thanked their Norse gods for the reprieve, while twenty-eight Christians praised Jesus.

At daybreak, the Vikings wandered along the shore and headed inland, where they came upon the grape vines Leif had spoken of. However, they soon realized they were actually gooseberries, but a welcome sight to see, nonetheless. As they picked and ate the berries, Thorfinn spotted a set of eyes between the branches. He pushed his way through and came face-to-face with a native. The young woman cowered as Thorfinn approached her, yet, with the use of hand signals and descriptive sounds, Thorfinn assured the woman he meant no harm. Despite the barrier, it was clear that the native likewise posed no threat. However, she conveyed that her tribe would not look upon their arrival so kindly.

Thorfinn released the young woman and returned to the beach, where he gathered the crew and said to all, "I ran into a native Skraeling. She appeared friendly enough, but I must tell you—we are *not* welcome here!" He glanced at Freydis. "It appears Leif was right." He gazed back at the entourage. "We set sail tomorrow."

Freydis sprang to her feet as the beads and two broaches on her strap dress rattled. "Thorfinn, we knew before setting sail what we'd encounter here! Any tribe in the world will resist foreigners who encroach upon their territory. It's the basic law of nature. We came here to find fertile land, land where we can grow crops, catch fish in bountiful seas, and raise families. And this place provides that, on all accounts." Gazing at her cohorts, she added, "I say we stay! What say all of you?"

The Vikings glanced uneasily at their comrades, then at Thorfinn, whose lips twisted with animus, as he spat, "Listen to me, Freydis! Leif may be your brother, but he entrusted *me* with this expedition. I won't tolerate a mutiny, especially by a shield-maiden!"

As the Vikings' eyes gazed anxiously at Thorfinn, then at Freydis, who, unlike the other women, aptly sported warrior dress, she replied, "Thorfinn, if you'll recall, Leif mentioned *my* name immediately after yours. And it's quite clear that he granted us this voyage due to *my* endless pleas. I have no desire to step on your toes, but my voice had carried significant weight and will continue to do so until my last breath!" Turning toward the throng of Vikings, she barked, "Speak up! Let your voices be heard!"

As many heads turned uncomfortably away from the quarreling pair or toward the ground, others nodded meekly in agreement, as one Viking, Snorri Thorbrandsson, boldly replied, "Freydis has a point, Thorfinn. It's no affront to you—she merely speaks the truth. At least about us being granted this voyage, as well as our desires to make a permanent settlement here." He glanced at his peers with confidence. "Let's face it, no matter how far west or south we sail, we're sure to run into hostile natives." His eyes returned to Thorfinn. "So, why shouldn't we stand our ground?"

Thorfinn's red face returned to its normal alabaster pallor as he contemplated each of their words. It wasn't easy having to contend with a woman with an unruly mouth—who also happened to be the sister of an eminent explorer and Chieftain—especially among an expedition of a hundred and five men and only fifteen women. He would have preferred smacking her hard across her insolent face, but her bloodline and, unfortunately, her salient words made doing so a bad choice. Therefore, Thorfinn bit his tongue, and replied, "Very well. We shall go inland tomorrow to seek a suitable spot. But I take no responsibility for this decision." Looking at Freydis, then at Snorri, he added, "For, if all fails, we know where the fault lies. So, get some rest—we leave at dawn."

With that, Thorfinn grasped his wife Gudrid's hand and escorted her to their tent. In the middle of camp, a small campfire crackled and burned as two Vikings stayed on watch. Taking turns at napping, one closed his eyes while the other stoked the fire. At 3:00 AM they switched, and the next night watchman paced back and forth for two hours. Finally, he sat down by the fire. Bored, he scratched his long, grisly beard, then honed the blade on his knife. He then placed it on his lap as he stared into the dwindling flames, when suddenly, he heard a rustling sound. Curious, he pivoted, only to have his face impaled with an arrow! It pierced through his cheek and embedded deep into his skull.

His shriek of agony startled the slumbering Vikings, who groggily attempted to gather their weapons. Meanwhile, the Skraeling rained down on them, emerging from the surrounding trees with knives and axes, while the arrows of hidden archers whizzed through the predawn air, slicing through leaves and branches before hitting their targets. As scores of Vikings scrambled to put on their armor, several were impaled by the projectiles, while others were ambushed from behind, as Skraelings either slit their throats or split open their heads with axes.

Amid the panic, Snorri was killed while strapping on his helmet, as an axe-wielding native chased after Gudrid. Many Vikings retreated to their longships, yet Freydis admonished them. "Why are you men running away from these worthless creatures? You can easily slaughter them like cattle!" Angrily, she glanced around her. "Give me a weapon, damn it! I'll show you how to fight!"

Amid the confusion and screams, only a handful heard her. Furious at no response, Freydis picked up Snorri's sword, sliced a Skraeling's neck, who fell dead to the ground, then dug her fingers into his bloody lesion. She smeared two red warrior stripes on each of her cheeks, then ripped open her strap dress and beat the sword against her meaty breast. Several Skraeling warriors gasped at her savage display, as she yelled, "Come here, you cowards in the night, so I may slice *your* throats!"

With that, Freydis charged toward them, swinging Snorri's bloody sword as she shrieked like a rabid tigress. With fear in their eyes, the Skraelings fled the beach and retreated into the woods, as twenty Vikings, emboldened by Freydis's bravado, joined her and charged after them.

Forty-five minutes later, as orange rays of sunlight pierced through the woven canopy of twisted branches and leaves, the Vikings halted their charge and returned to the camp site.

The sight was painfully dour. Only four Skraelings lay dead on the beach, while the corpses of twenty-five Vikings were cradled in the arms of their loved ones. Chills ran down their spines as tears flowed and mournful whimpers filled the morning air.

Thorfinn gazed at the dead bodies of his comrades and gritted his teeth. His eyes eventually landed on Snorri, one of the bravest men he ever knew. But then a volcanic wave of nausea came over him as his eyes finally landed on a horrific sight—it was the mutilated body of his beloved wife. Gudrid had almost made it to the safety of the longship, but the savage warrior had flung his axe, which lodged in the nape of her neck. Once she fell, the savage retrieved his hatchet and dashed into the woods, but not before he hacked her into pieces like a felled tree.

Thorfinn's lips quivered as he took a deep breath and gazed at Freydis. He knew no words were necessary, as he felt the despondent eyes of everyone on him. With over a fifth of their expedition slaughtered, along with his dear wife, it was clear: Vinland would *not* be their new home.

With heavy hearts, the Vikings erected a large funeral pyre on the beach. In silence, they watched their loved ones turn into ashes, whereby they drifted on the northerly winds, up to the esteemed summit of Valhalla. Some thirty yards away, five were buried according to their new Christian tradition, as their loved ones bowed their heads in prayer and beseeched their Lord to welcome the souls of the departed into Heaven.

At noon, they gathered around the campfire as three lambs and four turkeys roasted over a pit. It was time to finally broach the topic of their plans, and Thorfinn finally spoke. "Vinland, for many of us, shall now and forever be called Sinland. I grieve the loss of twenty-three stout men and two fine women—my own wife included. As Leif had warned, this land holds no place for us. I therefore propose we sail farther south along the shore to warmer climes."

Only the sounds of teeth gnawing lamb or turkey meat off bones could be heard, when Freydis uttered, "We all mourn the loss of our dead, Thorfinn, but Norse folk have never lived in warmer climes. And let me say this, during our charge this morning, I encountered a Skraeling in the woods—a young woman. She was not one of those who attacked us. She appeared timid, and naturally frightened. Being unarmed, she kept her distance, but tossed a map at my feet."

Thorfinn sat upright. "It sounds like the woman I had seen." He squinted. "What sort of map?"

Freydis lowered the lamb shank in her hand. "A map of an island, rich and fertile, with plenty of sea life in its waters." She glanced at her peers. "It's just a few days' journey from here. The Skraeling then motioned with her hands, indicating it would be a safe place for us to settle. It's called Slumber Mountain."

"Slumber *Mountain*?" Thorfinn said. "Are you sure it's an island?"

"Yes, look here," she said as she placed the chunk of lamb on her thigh and pulled the map out of her satchel. Eagerly, she unrolled it and turned it around for all to see.

On the parchment was an aerial drawing of an island surrounded with sharp, jagged mountains along its perimeter. Only one location offered access to the island, via an inlet. Next to this was a vivid illustration depicting the carved, colossal head of the peculiar Slumber god who protects the island's entrance. However, the Skraeling woman had told Freydis that only a handful of natives live there and pose no threat, so the bounty of the large island was theirs for the taking.

Thorfinn snorted as he almost gagged on the turkey bone. He wiped his mouth and cackled, "Ha! So, *she* told you they pose no threat, and that this island is a paradise, rich and fertile?" He glanced at his male companions and mockingly rolled his eyes at her, then added, "It appears your woman's intuition failed you, Freydis. What makes you think she was telling the truth? It sounds more like a trap to me."

Freydis smirked. "I guess anything *I* suggest is a mistake to *you*, Thorfinn. Did it ever occur to you that the Skraeling might just wish to make sure we find a settlement elsewhere, on a distant island where we won't interfere or slaughter them in retaliation?" With that, she stood up and heatedly tossed her half-eaten lamb shank into the fire. "Fine! I don't give a damn where we go." She turned toward the assemblage. "You can all decide amongst yourselves. I'll admit, I was wrong about Vinland, but we can't wait a moment longer. We must set sail *now*! So make up your damned minds."

She wiped the lamb grease off her lips, turned, and headed toward her longship. Without looking back, she boarded the vessel and disappeared into its shapely hull.

Amid the dead silence, Snorri's son, Einar, picked up his father's sword and declared, "Listen, one and all—Freydis defended my father's honor in battle, so I say, we go to Slumber Mountain. She may have been wrong about *this* place, but we mustn't forget—she has the noble blood of Leif Erikson in her veins." As many humbly nodded, he continued, "After all, she led a courageous charge this morning that turned what could have been a total massacre into a partial slaughter. Our survival is due to her gallant counterattack." His eyes glanced up at the heavens. "And I know my good father would have wished I follow in her footsteps."

Thorfinn tapped the turkey bone on his knee, as the fire crackled and glistened in the late morning air. As all sitting around the campfire awaited his response, Thorfinn finally nodded, reluctantly. "Yes, I have no doubts about Freydis's determination and abnormal strength for a woman, Einar. But, at times, her zeal tramples logic." He paused to pick the turkey bits out of his bushy mustache, then flicked them into the fire. He rinsed his mouth with a swig of ale. "Although I have reservations about a meek Skraeling recommending this mysterious island, Freydis *did* raise a sound point—Norsemen are not fond of warmer weather. So, yes," he paused, not relishing the next line. "I'll have to concur. We might as well make this crazy journey. Slumber Mountain it is."

With the sun perched at midday, the three Viking longships set sail into the Atlantic and sailed north into the icy waters. Two days later, they came upon an archipelago, as a thick fog rolled in over the surfeit of tiny islands. The Vikings squinted and grew restless; they could see that they were not full-fledged islands, but rather rocky spires, only an acre or so in size. They glanced at each other, disappointed and feeling deceived, when out of the fog, they saw a massive island emerge from the mist.

Freydis smiled. "That's it, all right! Look at those enormous mountains. I told you that native woman meant well."

As the longships approached, they came upon a series of razor-sharp rocks, which jutted out of the water like daggers. The Vikings gazed at the rocks' unnatural formations. They were intrigued, yet soon realized they posed perilous dangers, as the lead ship's hull was almost sliced open. Each of the three vessels' captains barked out the same command, and at eighty-yards away from shore, their ships drifted to a stop. Meanwhile, the mist had partially dissipated to reveal the freakish idol that gave the island its name.

Jaws dropped all around. Carved into the mountainous shoreline was the ghoulish Slumber Idol. It was enormous, and stood over a hundred and fifty feet tall. The Vikings gasped; they had never seen a statue of this size before as they peered at their sister ships then back up at the strange colossus. They were dumfounded at the sight; it dwarfed their longships, which appeared like toy models in comparison.

Although many Vikings knew that the Colossus of Rhodes had been hailed as one of the Seven Wonders of the World, it was clear: this unknown behemoth overshadowed that grand feat, perhaps not by its size, but more so by its eerie appearance and ominous portent.

As Thorfinn and his crew stared in wonder, a creepy feeling seeped into his bones—he was unnerved *and* confused. Thorfinn realized the Greeks had built their statue of the titan Helios to commemorate their victory at war, but was baffled by this peculiar monstrosity, with its part-beast, part-human face. More disturbing still, were the clawed fingers that protruded out of its ugly head.

Thorfinn turned toward Freydis. "What do you make of it?"

Freydis's eyes were still locked on the towering oddity. "I'm not sure," she said, still unable to free her eyes from the entrancing vision. "Although grotesque, its eyes are closed, which gives it a rather peaceful appearance."

She fondled with one of her long red braids—a habit she had since a child when deep in thought. "However, the sharp talons on its fingers are quite menacing." She finally peered at Thorfinn. "Perhaps they're meant to convey that this island is peaceful, unless provoked."

Thorfinn's nerves tingled as his unsteady fingers scratched his bushy mustache. "Well, Freydis. Although this idol slumbers, or perhaps meditates somewhat serenely, its beastly face and claws give me little hope that anything here is peaceful." His eyes scanned the strange island's coastline. "I have a bad feeling about this place."

Freydis glanced back at the colossus, then fixed her gaze on Thorfinn. "If *you* sought to guard your island from invaders, wouldn't you erect something scary to ward them off, like the gargoyles Christians put on their cathedrals?"

Thorfinn's intense gaze was broken as he looked at Freydis. "Yes, I suppose so. But—"

"So, we're here now. We might as well see what lies beyond this idol."

Thorfinn grasped a piece of salty, dried meat and chewed on it as he gave the matter more thought. He masticated the meat and wracked his brain for several minutes, then turned abruptly. To all, he broadcast loudly, "One of our longships will sail past the idol, into the inlet. Once there, they will reconnoiter the area, then return to report their findings."

Before Thorfinn could designate one of the ships, Einar—who had assumed command of his dead father's ship—volunteered. Without haste, he ordered his men to mount their lances and shields.

With a nod from Thorfinn, Einar's longship sailed slowly toward the mysterious idol. As they sailed past, his crew nervously gazed up at the sleeping monstrosity, expecting its stone eyelids to open at any moment, while the clawed hand on its head might snatch their tiny ship out of the water to devour them.

Amid sighs of relief, they passed the creepy gatekeeper without incident, while marveling at the sweet fragrance that permeated the air. With glee, they imagined all of the sweet fruits and aromatic herbs they'd soon find ashore. Einar's helmsman carefully steered the longship through the narrow mountain pass where they came upon a picturesque harbor, its shape matching the one on the map. Einar instructed his helmsman to remain aboard, while he and his twenty-eight crewmembers geared up and went ashore.

Wielding their swords, the Vikings climbed up a rutted path to the peak. From there, they gazed down upon a lush valley. Before their eyes was a golden meadow that sported exotic flowers, wheat, herbs, and a broad variety of trees that offered apples, pears, and an assortment of berries. Einar stood in awe as he scanned the horizon.

Filled with delight, his men were about to pick fruit to eat, when Einar waved his sword and motioned toward something in the distance.

Cautiously, they all stepped backward and crouched down, as their eyes zeroed in on Einar's objective. It was a small outpost with only five ramshackle huts. Sixteen unkempt villagers, with shabby clothes and archaic tools populated the settlement, among a healthy variety of livestock.

Einar looked at his fellow Vikings and smiled; he had fulfilled Thorfinn's instructions, and he ordered his reconnaissance team back to the ship. Yet as they headed back down the mountain pass, his men started to complain: eight had severe headaches, twelve were nauseous, nine already vomited, while ten others felt dizzy and collapsed. Einar blinked hard, as he too felt lightheaded. Concerned, he rubbed his forehead, then inspected those who had fallen. He felt their pulses. Einar's face went shockingly pale.

His men weren't just sick—they were dying, dropping dead at an alarming pace.

He, and the eight men still alive, dashed down the mountainside and back to the ship. As they struggled to climb aboard, Einar wheezed, "Return to the fleet, *at once!*"

The eight men quickly manned the oars while the helmsman turned the rudder and barked out rowing instructions. The ship turned and picked up speed, yet as the large vessel left the inlet, five oarsmen gagged and fell over dead, leaving only three to propel the ship. Slowly, they glided past the ghastly idol and out into the sea, as they slowly slid in between the two other longships. By then, the remaining three oarsmen had also collapsed and died.

Wet with fever, Einar called out to both ships with a choke and a gag, "My c-crew is d-dead! Save for us t-two."

Thorfinn clutched his heart. "The gods have abandoned us! I *knew* this place was cursed!" He glanced at Freydis with scornful eyes. "Damn it! I told you this was a bad decision!" He gazed at her as if she were Hel, the goddess of the underworld. *"You,* Freydis, will be the death of us! We must turn around and leave at once!"

Freydis squinted, deep in thought, as she pulled her red, wool cloak tight around her neck and then fumbled with her braid. As the wind blew across her face, she finally turned and retorted, "This doesn't make sense!" She peered over at Einar and called out, "Were you attacked?"

"No," he said with a gasp, as his heart fluttered in his chest. "We s-spotted a small v-village...only sixteen p-people, a primitive lot. We made no c-contact," he stuttered. "I d-don't understand. We ate n-none of the bountiful fruits and g-greens there. It's a b-beautiful place, just like the friendly Skraeling woman said. Plenty of l-livestock, too. But—" Einar grabbed his head and stomach as cold chills rankled his body. Falling to his knees, he gagged and stuttered, "This island l-looks and f-feels like p-paradise... I just d-don't un...der...sta—" Einar fell dead to the deck. Meanwhile, his helmsman had already died, his body hunched over the rudder.

Nervously, Freydis and Thorfinn lowered their heads with heavy hearts, as thoughts of the mysterious plague rattled their bones. With similar dread, the crews of the two remaining ships nervously rubbed their parched lips or scratched their disheveled hair.

Thorfinn felt numb as he gazed worriedly at the deck with a blank stare. He couldn't get the numbers out of his head; their original expedition of one hundred and twenty Vikings was now reduced to sixty-five. With each new catastrophe, their expedition was only proving that Leif had been right. And the fact that they had little to eat the past few days didn't help matters. With a deep sigh, he looked up and ordered twelve crewmembers from each ship to board Einar's ship and appointed a new captain.

Meanwhile, Freydis had been pacing the deck on her ship, when suddenly, she stopped and looked over at Thorfinn. "I still say it doesn't make sense. Why did Einar and his whole crew die when there are people living on the island?" Still fiddling with her long red braids, she deduced, "Therefore, it wasn't something they ate. It had to be something they touched or smelled."

Impelled by her own revelation, her eyes darted back toward the island. As they did, she realized that the idol's immense nostrils emitted a fine mist. Evidently, the fog that had earlier blanketed the archipelago had dissipated over the past two hours and now revealed the idol's vaporous emissions. Freydis's eyes widened. "Of course!"

Thorfinn shook his head, confused. "Of course *what*?"

Freydis pointed. "The nostrils, that mist... It must be poisonous!"

Thorfinn turned and gazed up at the monstrous idol's head that dominated Slumber Mountain. He squinted. "You might be right." He turned and looked at Freydis. "Yet, it's rather curious—I mean, how those sixteen natives are alive, with lots of food." He opened his marmot fur-lined cloak and rubbed his growling stomach as he peered back at the idol, intently. "If only there was a way to get past this deadly menace. My belly cries for a good harvest."

Several Vikings interjected with similar pleas for food, as one said, "We can die of starvation out here, Captain, or try our luck there. And since we now know there's plenty of food on this island, I say we give it a go!"

Thorfinn gazed at them, many of whom hadn't eaten a good meal since they departed in haste from Vinland. "Well, men, I wouldn't mind getting to those lush meadows myself, but you heard and saw what happened to Einar and his crew. Slumber Mountain poses a grave obstacle."

Nervously, his eyes veered up at the gargantuan idol. "Evidently, that poison gas spewing out of that ugly rock's nostrils is meant to put *us* into a deep slumber—*forever*."

Unexpectedly, Freydis stepped to the bow of her ship and called out for ten archers. As they assembled on deck, Thorfinn looked over at her vessel and squinted. "What in the name of Odin are you doing? It's a *rock*, you silly woman, not real!"

"Yes, *I know*," Freydis retorted. "The arrows aren't meant to kill it. With a bit of luck, they'll blow it up." With that, she ordered the archers to ignite the arrowheads and shoot them into the slumbering idol's nostrils.

Having grasped her scheme, Thorfinn looked on with admiration as the archers pulled back their bows and launched the flaming arrows.

As the fiery missiles sailed into the two cavernous targets, the flammable gas ignited! A massive explosion blew apart the deadly idol's nose. The force of the blow caused its entire face to collapse, as its sleepy eyes and gnarly forehead crumbled. Meanwhile, the large clawed fingers on its head wobbled and toppled over. They crashed on the rocky shoreline and cracked into huge shards, some of which tumbled into the sea. Within minutes, the dust and toxic mist subsided, and only a huge heap of rubble remained.

As the crews on each ship cheered, Freydis waved for silence. She asked for a single volunteer to scout the island. No one stepped forward.

Freydis feverishly pulled out her ironclad skirt and strapped it over her yellow dress. With a huff, she strapped on her scabbard, fitted with a Carolingian sword, giving her a distinctive and formidable aura, one that set her apart from all other Viking women. Heatedly, she bellowed for all to hear. "So, you Vi-*kings* all wish to eat the bounty of this island's glorious meadow and its livestock, yet not one of you is brave enough to pass that pile of rubble. Very well, you bunch of Vi-*kats*—*I'll* go!"

As waves of Vikings were shamed into volunteering, Freydis flipped her wrist. "Stand back!" she huffed. "I said I'd go."

With that, she climbed down into a raft and—with her uncommon strength—paddled toward shore. A frigid breeze blew across her face as she approached the huge pile of rocky debris. As she passed, her eyes carefully observed the fragments of the creepy idol: a portion of its thick lips here, a shard of its sleepy eyelids there, while three of its sharp talons protruded unnervingly out of the water, looking as if they might claw her raft, or any ship that attempted to pass.

Freydis took a deep breath, not only to calm her nerves, but also to test the air. With some relief, she didn't smell anything toxic, nor did she feel any malignant symptoms—at least not yet. She entered the secluded inlet and landed ashore. With determination, Freydis scaled the mountain pass. Yet, as she did, she came upon the dead bodies of her fellow Vikings. Freydis's throat tightened with grief as she stepped over them, recalling a familiar face here, a dear friend there, or those she and others had come to rely on. There was Jakob, the talented carpenter; Liam, the skillful blacksmith; Aksel, the hearty farmer; Sigurd, the valiant warrior. Her stomach turned, not in sickness, but with melancholy, as she closed her eyes and offered up prayers. With a deep breath, she resumed her journey and finally reached the apex of the mountain.

Not feeling any signs of poisoning, a sense of relief washed over her as she peered down into the lush valley.

Yet as she did, four native scouts spotted her. Blowing into their rams' horns, the chilling alarm reverberated throughout the valley. Freydis turned and made a dash to her raft, but they chased after her. As she raced down the mountainside, four natives overtook her and pinned her to the ground.

Meanwhile, an older native, more dignified than the rest, approached and stood over her. He gazed down into her eyes. "Why did you heathens destroy our peaceful idol, built to honor our God, Kognishen?"

Freydis squirmed to no avail as she spat, "Because your poisonous idol *killed* thirty of my fellow Vikings! That's why! And how can you honor a monstrosity that kills innocent people? We meant no harm."

The elderly native crossed his arms as he glanced at the sacred rubble in the distance, then back at Freydis with the gravity of an oracle. "Kognishen is a peaceful God, a loving God. Why do you think His image is in a state of slumber? He contemplates what is unknown to us, yet knows all. Yes, all of the world's secrets are held in the palm of His mighty hand, thus being a part of His head and pensive mind. Make no mistake, intruder, only *He* can enlighten us."

Freydis continued to struggle, frustrated, and still unable to repel the four young men pinning her down. Moreover, she didn't care to hear about this man's crazy cult. "I'm sorry, but I disagree," she growled through her teeth. "Those talons that sprung out of its ugly head were there to inflict death, not enlightenment!"

Unaffected by her insults, the elderly man smiled. "Young lady, you have it all wrong. As I said, those fingers represent the All-Knowing Hand—the hand that *grasps* the wealth of knowledge, which Kognishen contemplates in His meditative slumber."

Freydis stopped squirming, her breast still heaving from the chase and struggle. "If Kognishen is so brilliant, and grasps *all* knowledge, why doesn't He give it to you and your people?"

"What makes you think He doesn't?"

Freydis laughed as she raised her head and peered at their ramshackle huts in the distance, then back up at their shabby clothes. "Look at you, you're primitive, all of you. I see you haven't even learned to smelt bronze. We Vikings could show you many ways to advance your tribe, if you'll let me up."

The elderly man chuckled as he looked at his four scruffy underlings. "She seems harmless enough. Release her."

Freydis rose to her feet and brushed the dirt off her ironclad skirt. "You chuckled. Why? You don't think we can teach your tribe new techniques?"

"Of course you can't," he said smugly. "You're so primitive, you can't even realize when you're amid a superior race."

Freydis's lips twisted in contempt, but then she smiled. "Okay, perhaps I shouldn't have been so frank. I insulted you, and you retaliated in kind. But, I'm serious, my people *would* be willing to teach you various methods to improve your way of life."

He grasped her hand gently and asked for her name, which she offered, and he gave his. Aristen then smiled. "This isn't a matter of etiquette, Freydis. You see, our shanty hut and shabby clothes are decoys, meant to fool marauders, like yourself, who manage to get past our idol and its deadly protective fragrance. You happen to be the first and only ones to destroy our idol in doing so, which is a rather impressive feat, even if profane." As Freydis cracked a subtle smile of satisfaction, he continued, "Our primitive appearance is meant to lure trespassers into a false sense of superiority, so we can more easily predict and manage their mistakes, just like how we knew you'd return after destroying our idol. But now, allow me to show you our advanced society."

Freydis looked at Aristen and squinted as her brain raced to comprehend his provocative words. *Were they just a lie, or perhaps a deadly trap?*

As Aristen escorted her to the far side of the meadow, they came upon a line of tall conifers that stretched across the field, forming a huge barrier wall. In the middle was a narrow opening with a path, which extended only two hundred feet, whereupon it opened up to a sprawling city. As they reached the other side, Freydis was torn, being both dismayed—by her culture's lack of ingenuity—and amazed by the remarkable city before her.

The architecture was like nothing Freydis had ever seen or dreamt imaginable, featuring unique designs and advanced features built out of iron, stone, and wood, yet all maintaining a somewhat tribal aesthetic.

Aristen delighted in seeing Freydis's awestruck expression as he escorted her onto a hydraulic monorail. He explained how the metal cart with a thatched roof was propelled by confined water in heated conduits, which kept the water from freezing during the frigid winter months.

As it lunged forward, Freydis recoiled. Her head spun around. "You mean there are no horses or oxen to pull this cart?"

Aristen chuckled. "No, Freydis. As I said, we utilized the power of water to do various tasks that otherwise would have relied upon animals. As you're painfully aware, animals need to be fed, rested, cared for, and most importantly, they eventually die. Water never needs to stop to eat, never gets old, nor does it ever die, Freydis. So, as I told you, we are a very advanced society."

He pointed to a large, iron and wood-clad edifice, three-stories tall. "That building features multiple living quarters. Better yet, it has radiant heat and indoor plumbing." Aristen then pointed to a large, circular structure, which Freydis realized resembled images she had seen of Stonehenge. "Those precisely arranged stones keep an accurate track of time, as well as the seasons and constellations."

With each new marvel, Freydis felt more and more like a child. She gazed at the buildings and the natives strolling along the paved streets, many wearing exotic clothing, one more beautiful than the next. Aristen then showed her a plethora of bronze and iron instruments and gadgets of every kind: for navigation, agriculture, metalworking, carpentry, medical procedures, and more.

Freydis was overwhelmed into submission. However, amid her tour of the advanced society, Freydis had been perplexed by a glaring oddity. She had noticed that many of the Slumberians—which they called themselves—had only one leg. Compounding that oddity was when Aristen escorted her to the Grand Exalted Chieftain's royal palace and introduced her to Mono-Kundo, who also had one leg.

After their brief introductions, where Freydis made sure to reveal her own lofty roots and homeland, she inquired, "I must ask you, Mono-Kundo. Why do you, and so many of your people, have one leg?"

Mono-Kundo's congenial expression withered. "Such a question, Freydis from Greenland, must not be asked, as such matters are reserved for Slumberians only, *not* strangers." He adjusted his ornate headpiece, adorned with rare bird feathers and jewels, and regained his affable air. "If you wish to apply, and can prove yourself a loyal citizen for four months, then and only then will you be entitled to all our knowledge, knowledge granted to us by the good graces of our laudable God, Kognishen. If interested, proof of loyal citizenship only requires that you readily assimilate to our rich culture and be open to learning new trades. You may even retain your own religion. It's really quite simple."

Freydis was not only overwhelmed by the great city, but now also intrigued by the offer. "So, does that mean all sixty-five of us Vikings can join your Slumberian tribe?"

"Not *join*," Mono-Kundo corrected. "Apply. As I said, you all will have to pass our four-month probation period. After which, you will become a Slumberian. And that splendid day, I'm sure, will be cause for much celebration."

Freydis glanced at all the advanced gadgets and sophisticated buildings and recalled the lush vegetation and livestock. Slumber Mountain certainly offered everything they had set out to acquire. In fact, it was much more than she had dreamed of. Despite the unfortunate deaths of thirty Vikings, Freydis knew her expedition would benefit greatly by the Slumberians' advanced society. She also recalled how her father, Erik the Red, said that anything worth attaining in life often required bloodshed. Therefore, it was time to not look back on their misfortunes, but instead, look forward to the bright future that awaited them in this progressive and bountiful wonderland.

Freydis nodded. "This sounds most agreeable. Please allow me to return to my fellow Vikings to relay the good news."

Mono-Kundo smiled as he fiddled with the gold medallion of Kognishen on his vestments. "Enlightenment already permeates your spirit, I see. You may be excused.

And I am delighted by your wise decision." He glanced at Aristen. "Please escort her."

As they turned, Mono-Kundo added, "Oh, yes." They both stopped and pivoted around. "The first task several of your fellow Vikings will be given will be to rebuild our sacred idol. I hope that is agreeable?"

Freydis humbly bowed. "Yes, Mono-Kundo. It shall be done. All we ask is that we may collect the bodies of our fallen so that they may be eulogized and delivered up to Valhalla."

Mono-Kundo squinted. "What exactly is your process of delivery?"

"We build funeral pyres, Mono-Kundo, to burn and deliver their ashes up to Valhalla. So, I guess you can say, in streams of smoke."

Mono-Kundo nodded thoughtfully as he gazed at the floor, then redirected his eyes back to hers. "I believe we can accommodate that, Freydis. And I personally appreciate your interest in our community and look forward to the day when all Slumberians can throw a feast in your honor."

Freydis bowed and departed.

†††

Two hours later, Freydis returned to the grand city with Thorfinn, trailed by sixty-three Vikings. As they walked upon the immaculately maintained cobblestone streets, most were overwhelmed by the impressive city, while others found it hard to shake loose the deaths of their friends or loved ones. However, it didn't take long before the pangs of sorrow dissipated and they reaped the benefits of the Slumberians' extravagant culture. Many ate a rich variety of fruits, vegetables, and an assortment of meats and fish, including caribou, lamb, salmon and lobsters, or took heated mineral baths in posh basins, while others were instructed on how to build sophisticated gadgets, carriages, towering five-story buildings, or a variety of tools for numerous trades.

†††

On day six on Slumber Mountain, all sixty-five Vikings gathered in a large, secluded hall. As they all took their seats and filled their plates, Freydis stood up. "I asked everyone to gather here in private to voice any concerns they may have. Although our hosts have graciously welcomed us and overwhelmed us with their kindness and teachings, I have been told that some of you have minor grievances. Therefore, I think it's wise if we all share what we have learned."

Haviin stood up first. "May I speak?"

Freydis looked at him and nodded. "Of course," she said, as she took her seat.

Haviin grasped the broad collars on his new uniform, each with a large "S" embroidered on them, indicating his role as a supervisor. "As you all know, I've been appointed to supervise a crew of thirty Vikings to rebuild their idol. While there, I've seen Slumberians sharpening those rocky formations in the bay, which almost sliced open our hulls." He paused, then added, "It got me thinking—I doubt many seafarers travel along these desolate waters, so why is this island protected like a fortress? After all, they *welcomed* us."

Thorfinn stood up. "You make a sound point, Haviin. They told me it was to protect their precious culture from marauders. But as you say, how many travelers truly come to this remote part of the world? And must these defensive devices *kill* seafarers before knowing their intentions? Wouldn't a warning be more reasonable?"

One Viking called out, "Indeed it would! And personally, I don't like the smell of it, nor did thirty of our friends, who died by their idol's poisonous stink!"

Sareel stood up forcefully. "Well, if anyone has a gripe about their idol's poison gas, it should be *me*! My husband died from it. But perhaps you're all losing sight of what this place truly is," she said, as her vibrant blue eyes scanned the assemblage. "It's a radiant dream, a wonderland! I've already learned new techniques for sewing and embroidery, as well as how to cook a variety of new recipes." She patted her firm but plump belly. "Granted, I gained a few pounds, but who would ever want to leave here? Not me. So I understand their need to protect our new home from marauders, whoever they may be."

Thorfinn shook his head. "Sareel, I don't view us as marauders, do you? So what about others like us who only seek settlement without warfare? Must thirty Vikings, including your husband, be killed?"

Sareel lowered her head as she sat down, while Freydis finally chimed in. "I feel the most responsible for bringing us here." She stood up and glanced at all of them. "I admit, I was thunderstruck by all the wondrous things I had seen here, and that's why I asked you all to come along. So, I understand the allure of this special island. But perhaps we all should be more observant of what the Slumberians' motives truly are. I also suggest that we convene nightly, at least until we all feel secure and settled in our new homeland." As all nodded in agreement, she sat down and added, "So, eat your meals, have a good night's rest, and keep your eyes and ears open."

†††

Four days passed and the nightly sessions revealed very little for concern, as most Vikings were elated by their new experiences and spoke highly of their new Slumberian friends. Most of the evening conversations were filled with the litany of benefits the island offered, such as how the surrounding waters offered plenty of fishing; livestock on the island was robust and well maintained; new farming methods yielded far greater quantities and better quality vegetables and herbs, while Slumberian chefs offered up creative new dishes, with the only downside being that all of them had gained weight. But as seafarers accustomed to limited supplies at sea, gaining weight on land was to be expected. In fact, most said the past several days had been the best in their lives.

On the eleventh evening, everyone took their seats with great satisfaction—until, that is, Freydis marched in and kicked off the meeting with an ominous hammer blow, akin to that of mighty Thor. "I know you've all found happiness here, and a fabulous new home. But what I'm about to reveal, I'm sure, will change your minds."

All sixty-four Vikings sat with bated breath while Freydis continued, "As I have told you, Mono-Kundo said he would allow us to deliver our dearly departed to Valhalla. However, as you also know, they had taken the bodies and told us they were keeping them on ice until we completed rebuilding the idol. What I discovered, however, will come as a shock." Her radiant green eyes scanned the faces of her beloved people, as she said with a heavy heart, "We will no longer have the honor of performing the funeral pyre service. They have betrayed us!"

92

As Thorfinn, Sareel, and countless others gasped, fearing their friends and loved ones might never reach the laudable halls of Valhalla, Freydis relayed a far greater insult. "I've been informed of this blasphemy by Haviin. While rebuilding the idol, he discovered a large, sacred chamber beneath the structure." She swallowed hard, pained to even utter the following line. "The Slumberians have already burned the bodies of our loved ones—yet not on a funeral pyre, but rather in a large, boiling vat mixed with poisonous herbs and incense."

Many Vikings rose in anger, as Thorfinn sprang to his feet and punched the table, so hard that his goblet fell over. "The bloody bastards! Defiling our dead like this is an outrage!"

As others echoed his anger, Sareel's voice resonated loudest, as she demanded in denial, "But why? For what purpose would they boil them?"

Freydis waved for silence. As their voices quieted, she said, "I must warn you all, this cult's procedures are most disturbing, as is its ultimate purpose. What befell our loved ones has happened to countless others before us." As all in the hall gazed at Freydis with their hearts in their mouths, she went on, "The Slumberians concoct a vile mixture of human bodies and poisonous herbs and disguise its foul odor with incense. When poured over hot sulfur it becomes a deadly gas, yet with a sweet aroma. That beguiling fragrance happens to be the toxic mist that emanated out of their idol's nostrils." Her head lowered. "I also learned that the human fatty oils prolong the burning, so a very small amount burns for days."

Sareel covered her mouth and almost vomited, while several others pushed themselves away from the table and kicked over their chairs. Eyes rolled in disbelief and stomachs twisted with disgust, as Freydis added, "That's why they're anxious for us to rebuild their hideous idol. The innocent deaths of our fellow Vikings will be used to cause more innocent deaths, while never being granted access to Valhalla—the ultimate sacrilege."

Voices of vengeance mounted and echoed throughout the chamber, when Freydis suddenly banged the table with her empty goblet. As the attention of her audience was restored, she continued, "There is more—much more that will boil your blood, just as they have boiled our loved ones. We have indeed entered the dark underworld of Hel. For the Slumberians are grooming us all to be sacrificed, some to be boiled for their poisonous idol, others to be fed and fattened, only to be eaten at their sacrificial feast."

Many gasped and shifted in their chairs, while those standing couldn't believe their ears.

"This is madness!" one bellowed, while another interjected, "This just can't be. You must be mistaken?"

Haviin finally stood up. "What she says is true! I've seen the boiled bodies myself and overheard their plans for our sacrifice, like lambs to the slaughter." As the naysayers looked on in stunned silence, Haviin continued, "Their sacred chamber dwells deep under their idol's massive head, and it is there that they carry out their rituals. I also discovered why Mono-Kundo and so many Slumberians have only one leg." As the crowd hushed to near silence and all eyes fixed on Haviin intently, he continued his dark tale.

"Six years ago, the Slumberians had experienced a shortage of visitors whom they could offer up as sacrifices, or as fuel for their idol's poisonous brew. As such, Kundo offered his own leg as sacrifice to Kognishen, which explains his present name—*Mono*-Kundo." As his fellow Norsemen glanced at each other in shock, then back at him, he went on,

"Despite his offering, however, eighteen months had passed and no visitors arrived to be sacrificed. Therefore, Mono-Kundo decreed that one citizen per month had to sacrifice a leg to appease their god."

As the Vikings listened in disbelief, Freydis once again took charge. "It's bizarre and morbid, yes. But now that the Slumberians have sixty-five fattened Vikings at their disposal, they can rejoice in offering years of sacrifices to Kognishen, while also providing themselves with hundreds of pounds of human meat, meat they intend to eat at the end of our four-month probation period at the *feast* Mono-Kundo said was in our honor."

Thorfinn had heard enough and exploded. "That deceitful bastard!" He gazed at his fellow Vikings. "A feast to *honor* us! Ha! Mono-Kundo will pay dearly for those beguiling words!"

"Indeed he shall!" one Viking barked, to an echo of similar refrains.

Meanwhile, Sareel looked on in a daze as she shook her head. Finally, she looked over at Freydis as a tear streamed down her pale cheek. "How people can sacrifice humans and even their own legs to their god is beyond my understanding, Freydis. It's insane!"

Freydis reached over and empathetically grasped her hand. "It certainly defies any logic we're accustomed to, Sareel." Peering out the window at the grand city, she went on, "Especially since they've managed to create such an advanced society." Solemnly, she glanced at Thorfinn, knowing it was time to acknowledge his wisdom. "Thorfinn had reservations upon our first sighting of their idol. It should have offered us all a warning."

Thorfinn slumped back into his chair, as feelings of regret mixed with frustration now tore at every fiber of his being. His head lowered in shame. "In that regard, I'm partly to blame for our folly, Freydis. I should have stuck to the lessons of observation that served me so well in the past." He raised his head and leaned forward. "What I've learned is, higher cultures often erect statues of laudable gods or heroes. Yet savages often worship that which lurks in the darkness of their hearts."

Haviin pulled his Carolingian sword out of his scabbard and stood on his chair. "I say we slaughter Mono-Kundo and these savages, right now!"

As some forty-odd Vikings unsheathed their swords or battle-axes, Freydis cried out, *"No!* We are vastly outnumbered, and will only meet the same fate that they planned for us if we act on impulse."

Thorfinn rose to his feet. "She's right. Put down your weapons! We must act upon the logic of our vibrant minds, not the impulse of our vengeful hearts."

Freydis's eyes oscillated to the tempest of thoughts in her head, while Thorfinn continued to tame the beasts in his men's angry hearts. For over an hour, their tumultuous discourse echoed throughout the hall amid the flickering glow of candlelight, then finally tapered off. Freydis then stood up and called for their attention. With all eyes on her commanding presence, she relayed her scheme. All agreed, and the plot was set in motion.

††††

Over the ensuing days, the Vikings resumed their normal, daily activities: they tilled the soil in the fields; smelted iron ore at the blacksmith's shop; built houses, carriages, or a variety of products—all without revealing the slightest bit of discontentment or mistrust. As planned, reconstruction of the Slumber idol had intentionally moved at a slower pace, its completion date not expected for another three months. This delay gave the Vikings ample time to execute their covert tasks. Freydis maintained her gracious and humble rapport with Mono-Kundo and Aristen, while all the Vikings upheld their façade of friendship and gullibility.

Meanwhile, the Slumberians eyed-up their blossoming, human crops of food and sacrifice with great delight—some even discreetly feeling their enlarged waists or arms while instructing them on new tasks, such as how to ride their two-wheeled invention called a bi-wheeler.

By the ninth day of the plot, the Vikings had managed to complete their preliminary tasks ahead of schedule, and Freydis anxiously met up with Haviin. The time had come— he was to enact her plan the following day, after work.

The next day, Haviin watched his construction crew closely as they finished their daily grind on the idol, while ensuring that the eighty-seven Slumberian stone-carvers and three supervisors didn't get suspicious. Amid the amber glow of twilight, the Vikings packed their belongings, said goodnight, and duly left the worksite. Several steps away, Haviin, along with five cohorts, ducked behind bushes where they had hidden six large buckets, and waited twenty minutes for the Slumberians to lock up and leave.

In preparation, Haviin had instructed Jurgon—a Viking blacksmith—to make a copy of a key, which Haviin had managed to swipe the day before, when a Slumberian supervisor wasn't looking. He had pressed the key into a clay mold and returned the key to the supervisor's leather pouch, undetected. Jurgon had poured molten bronze into the mold, and then gave the key to Haviin, who now opened the gate.

Cautiously, he stepped into the chamber inside the idol's massive head. The six Vikings moved at a snail's pace in the pitch dark as they stealthily crept to the concealed trap door. Haviin opened it and they crawled down into the sacred chamber, which was eternally lit with twelve large wall torches and a string of sanctified candles.

Their eyes widened as waves of nausea washed over them. Despite the pleasant fragrance, it was where the Slumberians stored the large vat of boiling bodies. The Vikings themselves boiled with rage, yet were oddly impressed at how well the fragrant herbs concealed the stench. Reluctantly, they leaned over and peered at the poisonous brew, brew made from their dear friends who would never reach Valhalla. Tears streamed down their cheeks as they filled their buckets with the deadly, hot liquid. Yet, Haviin reminded them to take solace in knowing that their friends' deaths would not be used to poison innocent visitors. Instead, their essence would be used to kill those who had killed and desecrated *them*, and enacted an evil plot to kill the remaining Viking expedition for both food and sacrifice.

As Haviin led his five saboteurs back up, a Slumberian guard unexpectedly appeared! Amid the darkness, he drew his sword and impaled one of the Vikings, then another. Quickly, he reached for his ram's horn to sound the alarm, but Haviin grabbed his head from behind and snapped his neck. The guard fell dead to the ground.

Haviin and the three surviving Vikings dragged the body back down below and tossed it into the boiling vat. Then, with sorrowful hearts, they retrieved their two dead comrades, locked the gate, and carried them, and the buckets of poison, to a secluded spot, where they covered the bodies with branches. They would be collected later when they fled the island, to be cremated honorably.

It was now time to complete their original mission. Haviin and his three accomplices each grabbed two large buckets of poison and carried them to the city's principal cistern. Nervous and out of breath, they each stood by the edge and peered down into the large tank. Haviin looked up at his cohorts and nodded as eight large buckets of death flowed into the sparkling water.

Stealthily, the four saboteurs dashed through the night on off-beaten paths and returned to their domiciles. Panting and with adrenaline surging through their bodies, they each tried to fall asleep, but couldn't. Hours passed, as they tossed and turned, tormented by the gruesome deaths of their fellow Norsemen, including the two brave compatriots that very night.

As the dawn's warm glow illuminated Haviin's room, an anxious Freydis burst through the door to greet him. Impatiently, she sat on the chair next to his bed and prodded him for the details.

Haviin sat upright and rubbed his bloodshot eyes. Freydis didn't like his rusty orbs or his somber expression.

With a sigh, he uttered, "Two more Vikings are dead."

Freydis bowed her head, but then quickly grasped his arm. "But, were you successful?"

"Yes. It is done. Just as you planned."

Freydis sighed as she slouched in her chair. She now knew it was only a matter of time before all the Slumberians fell into their own eternal slumber. The sweet taste of revenge soothed her as she thought of all the horrors exacted upon them by these deranged animals, monsters who prayed and sacrificed to a bizarre god. She thought of Odin and her Norse gods, those of the Greeks, the single God of the Jews, Christians, and Muslims, and the defunct gods of the Egyptians. Then, once again, her mind wandered back to this evil and warped god, whom they called Kognishen. None of it made much sense to her, but she at least found comfort in the tradition of her father's gods—unlike her brother, who had abandoned them to become a Christian.

Her reverie was shattered, however, when Thorfinn burst into the room in a state of panic. "By the gods, Haviin! What have you done?"

Haviin's weary eyes widened. "What do mean?"

Simultaneously, Freydis sprang up. "What's wrong?"

Thorfinn looked over his shoulder at the door. "I hope I wasn't followed, but we must flee this cursed island, immediately!"

Freydis grasped Thorfinn's scruffy face with both her hands. "Speak! Tell us what happened?"

His jittery eyes tried to focus on her face, as they still periodically shot back at the door. "Two royal guards are combing Viking homes as we speak, looking for the culprit, or culprits." He swallowed hard. "Rumor has it that they found drips of poison near the cistern. We've been found out! Your plan was a failure, Freydis! We're doomed!"

"Hold on!" Freydis said forcefully, as she clutched his face tighter. "Get a hold of yourself. You're a man of reason, remember? Calm down."

Thorfinn took several deep breaths and nodded. "Yes, yes, of course," he said as his hands still trembled. "But we must alert the others and flee as fast as we can."

"Not yet," Freydis advised. "Let's not jump to conclusions. Word of this may not have spread as far and quickly as you think. I'll head up to the royal palace to see what Mono-Kundo and Aristen truly know." She released her grip on his face and turned toward Haviin. "Hunt down those two royal guards immediately, before they spread the alarm. Go!"

With that, Haviin quickly strung his puttees around his legs, slipped on his shoes, and raced out the door. Meanwhile, Freydis pulled her red, woolen cloak tight around her neck and was about to follow, when Thorfinn nervously inquired, "Hold on! What shall *I* do? Just wait here for you to return…*if* they don't kill you, that is?"

"They won't kill me," Freydis said confidently. "Even if they know about our plot, that doesn't mean all of us were in on it. I'll simply deny knowing anything about it."

Thorfinn nodded mechanically. "Yes, of course." Doubt gripped him once again. "But what if—"

"Never mind, you're overthinking this," she chided. "Start spreading the word to our people that the plot has been discovered. They must prepare to leave immediately!"

With that, Freydis bolted out the door and headed toward the royal palace. As she raced through the cobbled streets, her long, red braids and crimson cloak flapped in her wake as the golden glow of the morning sun started to illuminate the city. When she approached the palace, she unexpectedly came upon Aristen, who was walking up the large flight of stairs to the main entrance.

Freydis came up beside him and offered him a pleasant smile. "Good morning, Aristen. Is Mono-Kundo awake?"

As he replied, Freydis scrutinized his every move and inflection. "Actually, I just arrived myself, Freydis. Let's go see."

Freydis couldn't detect anything nefarious in his demeanor, yet she also wasn't sure how good of a liar Aristen was. With that, Freydis nervously followed him into the building's main lobby, where a royal guard greeted them. "Good morning, Lord Aristen." He merely glanced at Freydis, and didn't offer her any recognition, as he added, "You're here rather early. Please have a seat, the Grand Exalted Chieftain is still getting dressed."

The guard retreated down the main corridor, while Freydis and Aristen took their seats in the lobby. Freydis tried her best to make small talk, but her mind wandered. *Is Aristen just playing along, like I am? Perhaps he and Mono-Kundo know already?* She glanced down the hall. *And that guard was pretty rude. Is this a trap?*

As she struggled to pull words from his mouth, she suddenly realized that her ploy of playing the innocent foreigner might be harder to pull off than originally expected. After all, their entire water system had been poisoned—on her instructions, no less—and any minute, alarms and hysteria would spread like the plague. Sweat moistened her forehead as her usually pleasant face morphed into an awkward stare.

Aristen squinted. "Are you feeling all right, Freydis? You look shaken, and uncommonly nervous."

"No!" she blurted. "I mean, no, not at all...why should I be?" she said, forcing a smile back on her face.

"It's just that I've never seen you sweat before, and with the temperature being on the cool side, I'm just concerned. I hope it's nothing serious."

Just then, Mono-Kundo appeared. "Good morning to you both." He gazed out the window at the sunlit trees and sparkling lake. "What a glorious day." He turned toward them as he buttoned up his bejeweled vest. "So, what brings you both before me at this early hour?"

Aristen glanced at Freydis. "You go ahead. I have much to discuss with the Chieftain, and I'm afraid I'll probably consume a large share of his morning."

Freydis nodded and looked at Mono-Kundo. "Well, I w-was just wondering," she stammered, "would it be—"

Suddenly, a whistle blew, interrupting Freydis as a loud ruckus erupted outside the palace. Mono-Kundo and Aristen recoiled, as Freydis's mind raced. *They've been caught! I'm dead! We'll all be executed!*

"Excuse us," Mono-Kundo said, as he hobbled out onto the terrace on his crutch, followed by Aristen. Freydis cringed as adrenaline ran through her. Slowly, she edged herself toward the door and peered out.

To her relief, the uproar was between a royal guard and Aristen's wayward fourteen-year old son, Zann-Kim, who was cussing the guard. "Keep your filthy paws off of me, you big lummox! I told you my pa is Lord Aristen!"

Meanwhile, the guard held Zann-Kim firmly by the nape of his neck and said, "I apologize for the disturbance, Grand Chieftain, but Zann-Kim insisted I bring him here. I caught him drinking, but worse yet, he bludgeoned a young girl, so forcefully that she's near death."

Aristen's nostrils flared like an enraged bull's. "Zann-Kim! I told you countless times, you are *not* entitled to special treatment because of my position. What's this all about?"

Zann-Kim snarled at the guard. "This dumb caribou had no business butting into a feud between me and my girlfriend. And the bitch *will* live, Papa, so don't worry."

Aristen gazed at Mono-Kundo and bowed his head. "I must apologize. Do what you will with him. He asked to be brought here, so let the axe fall where it may."

Zann-Kim gazed at his father in shock as Mono-Kundo shook his head, disappointed. "Zann-Kim, your father is right. We offer no special treatment to *anyone*. And—"

"Nonsense!" Zann-Kim interjected. "That's only because you have no kids and no family. If you did, you would. So, let me go!"

Aristen erupted. "Shut your mouth, you insolent fool! You're speaking to the Grand Exalted Chieftain!"

Mono-Kundo would have reprimanded Zann-Kim far more severely, but he still had to maintain his aura of dignity in front of his foreign guest, at least for now. "Zann-Kim, my lack of family plays no role in my decision, as we *all* must abide by the honorable and just Slumberian Laws."

Twenty years ago, Mono-Kundo's ancestors had established the draconian laws two months before being massacred by rebels seeking freedom from tyranny. In response, Mono-Kundo ordered his secret police to hunt down and slaughter the rebels, their bodies boiled in sacrifice. Although the Slumberian Laws offered considerable liberties, the atrocities occurred on the backend, for breaking even the most trivial of laws was met with severe punishment or death.

Mono-Kundo's expression turned gravely serious as he continued, "I offer Slumberians many freedoms, Zann-Kim, which they rightfully praise me and my ancestors for, yet only fools take that kindness for granted. If they abuse those freedoms, they insult *me*! And beating that girl almost to death is not something I can take lightly."

Zann-Kim stood mute as the hate behind his eyes welled. Meanwhile, Mono-Kundo continued his lecture and final sentencing, undeterred. "As you know, beating an unruly woman is acceptable by law, Zann-Kim. However, you exceeded the tolerable limit. As such, the axe indeed must fall. If it had been a man you struck, you would have been put to death. Fortunately for you, it was only a woman. Therefore, according to the laudable Slumberian Laws of this land, you must lose the hand that committed the offense." He gazed at the guard. "Check his knuckles, the bruised hand must go!"

Zann-Kim yelled and squirmed, but to no avail, as the guard dragged him to the terrace railing, placed his right hand on it, and swiftly chopped it off. Zann-Kim shrieked in agony as blood spurted from the wound in all directions.

Matter-of-factly, the guard removed an official Slumberian bandage from his pouch and dutifully wrapped Zann-Kim's bloody stump.

Mono-Kundo's lips twisted as he looked at his soiled railing, then at the guard. "Clean this mess up, then escort Zann-Kim to the infirmary."

Dutifully, the guard complied, then dragged Zann-Kim away, as his whimpers lingered in the morning air.

Freydis swallowed hard as an uncomfortable wave of anxiety came over her. With the customary hearing, sentencing, and punishment completed, Mono-Kundo nonchalantly turned toward Freydis. "So, what was it you wished to speak to me about?"

Freydis gently shook her head. "Never mind, I see you have a busy morning, Grand Chieftain." She glanced at Aristen, then back at the savage tyrant. "I'll call upon you some other time, if that's acceptable?"

"Very well, you may be excused," he replied. He then turned toward Aristen, and they both reentered the royal palace.

Freydis sighed and made a mad dash back to Haviin's domicile. Without knocking, she burst through the door and came face-to-face with him and ten other Vikings, including Thorfinn, who exclaimed, "By the glory of the gods, you were right! Haviin did as you instructed, with much success."

Freydis wiped her sweaty brow as she looked at Haviin, then glanced at his death squad. "How many guards did you have to eliminate?"

"Only two," Haviin said.

Freydis's tense shoulders relaxed.

He added, "However, we also had to silence the fourteen Slumberian citizens they alerted."

Freydis's head dropped. "How do we explain all these deaths?"

Haviin shrugged. "Not sure, but they're all going to start dying soon enough once they drink the water. So does it really matter?"

"Yes, Haviin," Freydis said. "At least for the time being, because they'll expect *those* deaths to be some type of sickness or plague. Meanwhile, *these* sixteen deaths were coldblooded murders. What did you do with all the bodies?"

He glanced at his cohorts. "Well, we dragged them into the bushes or threw them into ditches."

Freydis nodded thoughtfully. "I reckon that will have to suffice." She paused briefly as her luminous green eyes shifted in thought, then reaffixed themselves on Haviin's face. "I suggest you gather your entire crew and head for your ship. If anyone stops you, say your ship needs its usual maintenance repairs. After all, it *has* been sitting idle for weeks."

"Indeed it has," Haviin said. "And I can't wait to get the Hel out of here!"

With that, he motioned to his team and they exited, leaving only Thorfinn behind, who looked at Freydis. "I must say, you have handled this crisis very well. I apologize for my earlier misgivings. You have the makings of a first-rate leader, Freydis. Your brother will be proud."

Freydis managed to crack a smile. "Thank you, Thorfinn, but this crisis is far from over. I'm not sure what their reactions will be once they start dropping dead like flies while we Vikings remain standing."

Thorfinn paused in thought, then actually managed to chuckle as he quipped, "Well, we could tell these haughty bastards it's due to our *superior* blood!"

Freydis chuckled, but soon returned to her thoughts and her old habit of fiddling with her braids. She gazed back at Thorfinn. "This godforsaken island should be razed so no other travelers set foot on this cursed land."

Thorfinn shook his head. "Never mind that. We need to flee this place immediately. Let their rotting corpses and bones be enough of a warning to travelers that this place is cursed."

Freydis nodded. "I suppose you're right. Let us begin the exodus!"

As they raced and alerted their fellow Vikings, they all observed the startling results of Freydis's plot. Slumberians filled the streets in panic as they gasped, choked, and vomited. Soon, scores of Slumberians fell dead to the ground as hysteria gripped the city and pandemonium escalated. Meanwhile, the Vikings were gathering their belongings and fleeing at intermittent intervals toward the harbor, while Freydis and Thorfinn stayed behind to ensure the exodus was successful.

Just then, three middle-aged Slumberians ran toward them—their noses bleeding and foam oozing from their mouths—as one grabbed Freydis by the arm. "Why aren't *you* sick?" He glanced at Thorfinn, and the last remaining Vikings who were running toward the harbor, and gritted his bloody teeth. "*None* of you are sick!" He squinted. "You bastards did this! Didn't you?"

With the verdict now clear in his mind, the man lunged at Freydis. With venom and death running through his veins, the man wrapped his vengeful hands around her neck. Freydis choked and punched him in the solar plexus, causing the man to keel over and drop to his knees. The man coughed and gasped for air as he looked up, then spit at her face. Freydis kicked him hard in the chest and watched as his body flew backward and hit the pavement.

She wiped the man's bloody spit off her face, then turned toward Thorfinn, who just finished slashing another Slumberian who had attacked him. They both turned and ran, while other Slumberians caught on to the plot. Word spread fast, and soon hordes of Slumberians raced after the fleeing Vikings toward the inlet.

Leading the pack was Aristen, who took a shortcut through the woods and caught up to Freydis, whom he tackled to the ground. "You deceitful bitch! *You* did this—I know it!" He slapped her hard across the face. "I knew by your sweaty face this morning that something was afoot!"

Freydis kneed him in the groin and rolled on top of him, pinning his shoulders to the ground. "You dare call *me* deceitful? You and your deranged tribe intended to sacrifice and eat us!"

To Freydis's surprise, Aristen ceased struggling. His brown eyes, now tinged with emotion, gazed up into hers. "I grew to like you, Freydis—a great deal. Allow me to help you. I can persuade Mono-Kundo to offer you special treatment—a full pardon!"

Freydis looked down into his eyes and snickered. "I saw how Mono-Kundo offered your own son special treatment—by chopping off his hand. No, Aristen, the whole lot of you are sick, and this was the only way I knew how to end it."

Aristen twitched as his blood began to rise. "That's *not* true, Freydis! My son is a troublemaker—unfocused and expendable. But you, Freydis, are a leader. One we could use to head our forthcoming expedition to the mainland to expand our empire. It's not too late, Freydis. You see, Mono-Kundo and I didn't drink any water this morning. So we *will* prevail. And I will lie for you and defend your honor...I promise!"

With that, Freydis stood up, which elicited a smile from Aristen as he sat upright. "You won't regret this, Freydis."

Yet what Aristen heard next was not a concession, but the sound of her sword as it slid out of her scabbard.

His eyes bulged, as Freydis said, "Thank you for telling me Mono-Kundo wasn't poisoned. My work here is not yet done."

"B-but wait!" he stammered, "I s-said I would stick up for you. I promise!"

"And I'll gladly *stick you* with my blade. I promise!"

With that, Freydis rammed the blade deep into his chest. Aristen gazed at her in shock as he grasped the bloody blade. Freydis placed her foot on his chest, then pulled the sword out. Aristen's eyes rolled as his body fell backward into the tall grass.

By then, Thorfinn had backtracked, and now stood before the bloody corpse and the valiant redheaded slayer. "I was going to ask if you were all right, but I see that's quite obvious." He smiled. "You're one hell of a woman, Freydis, better than any man I have ever served in battle with, and I'm damn proud of you!"

Freydis truly appreciated the compliment, having won Thorfinn's respect, something she had long yearned for. However, she had no time for pleasantries, as she informed him, "Mono-Kundo is alive." Dutifully, she wiped the blade clean on her red cloak. "You go ahead. Make sure two of our ships are fully loaded to set sail. I'll meet up with you in thirty minutes. If I'm not there, ship out without me."

Freydis turned and started to run, while Thorfinn yelled out, "By the gods, leave him be! We must leave this place, *now!*"

"Not happening. Thirty minutes!"

Thorfinn shook his head with a half smile. He about-faced and headed toward the longships, but met with an arrow instead. It pierced right through his chest.

Freydis heard the *whoosh* of the arrow and Thorfinn's distinctive grunt. She stopped and spun around. Her heart raced as she looked at Thorfinn on the ground, then peered over her shoulder at the royal palace in the distance. She gritted her teeth and started toward Thorfinn, when a Slumberian guard jumped out of the woods and stood over him. With a flash of iron, his blade slit Thorfinn's throat.

Freydis ran up behind the guard and, with a mighty *whack*, decapitated him in one fell swoop. Adrenaline numbed her whole body like a drug as she turned and knelt down over her dear commander's carcass. With her heart pounding, she took a deep breath, regretting not acknowledging his kind words, words she had so longed to hear. Reverently, she closed her eyes, kissed her fingers, then placed them on Thorfinn's rigid face.

She opened her eyes and glanced back at the royal palace. As she rose to her feet, her ironclad skirt and beads rattled, akin to the iron resolve that now ran through her veins. With a primal grunt, Freydis resumed her mission.

Dashing through the streets—littered with the corpses of poisoned Slumberians, and those still staggering and vomiting blood—Freydis flew like the wind as her long, red braids and cloak rippled in the wind. Along her journey, she slashed attackers or hurdled over corpses, and finally made it to the palace, as she charged up the stairs and through the front door.

Mono-Kundo's eyes widened as she approached him. Wielding her mighty Carolingian sword, she stopped roughly twelve feet away from the tyrannical Chieftain. His face illuminated with rage. "How dare you come into *my* palace? You're nothing but a destroyer of a great civilization!"

Freydis ominously tapped her palm with the flat part of her blade. "This might have been a great civilization, Mono-Kundo, if it were judged only by the progress you made. But as for the heartless and deranged customs of your flesh-eating cult, you're nothing but savages, just like your hideous idol."

Once again, Freydis approached him, this time slowly as she swung her sword in graceful, swirling 'S' shapes, savoring the impending kill. As far as she was concerned, this delusional despot had probably killed thousands of innocent people, and his demise had to be memorable: a gory milestone to warn future tyrants of the cost for wielding evil.

"So, *Grand Exalted Chieftain*, you like dismembering people," Freydis said. "The hands of criminals, the bodies of innocent travelers, or your own citizens' legs to feed your blood-thirsty idol, a warped sacrifice that even *you* did to yourself. Well, allow me to assist you further!"

The next five minutes were the most horrific of Mono-Kundo's life as he learned the agonies of all the sadistic tortures he had practiced—only this time, firsthand.

Freydis dashed out of the palace and through the city of death, when, to her surprise, she came upon Haviin, who sighed with relief as he held a lit torch in the morning sun.

"What are you doing here?" she exclaimed. "You and your crew should have been long gone by now."

"Don't worry, I sent them off, they'll be fine." Haviin's eyes glistened with reverence and joy. "But how could I ever leave you behind, our fearless leader?"

Freydis smiled in gratitude, as Haviin's grin mellowed into a stiff upper lip. "I saw what they did to Thorfinn." He reached into his leather quiver, which was stocked with twenty arrows with flammable tips, and drew one out. He looked back up into her eyes and handed her the torch. "Would you mind doing the honors?"

Freydis nodded in approval. "I'd be delighted."

With that, she lit the tip of the arrow, and Haviin launched it high into the air, whereupon it eventually landed in the thatched roof of Mono-Kundo's royal palace. Haviin withdrew another arrow, which Freydis once again lit, and he sailed it into the administration building. The duo repeated the firing sequence like clockwork, and set the whole city ablaze.

As buildings burned, trees crackled, and the putrid smell of thousands of Slumberian bodies being roasted filled the air, Freydis and Haviin surveyed their handiwork, and then glanced at each other. The city of sin and perversion was duly eradicated.

Freydis winked, then they turned and headed for the harbor. They dashed through the meadow, down the mountain pass, and eventually reached the inlet. Two longships had already set sail, while the third sat placidly afloat in the rippling water, awaiting their arrival.

Freydis and Haviin boarded the ship, as the helmsman turned the rudder. To the sound of rhythmic chants, the oarsmen churned up a wake, while the unfurled sail billowed with wind. Slicing though the waves, the longship exited the inlet, as the crew's eyes gazed up at the Slumber Mountain idol. Once ominous and bloodthirsty, it was now a ruin, half unfinished, and just a dead relic of an ugly past, one to be forgotten.

An hour later, they had caught up to their two sister ships, and the three Viking vessels continued their journey together. However, this time it was not into the unknown, but rather back home, never to explore the New World again, as that would be left to more courageous and willful souls... For the Vikings sunny days of exploration had irrevocably set.

REFLECTIONS of CONQUEST

They came in the night.

It was on December 25, 2525, five years ago, when three spaceships landed. Many Christians believed it to be the long-awaited return of Christ; being that it was on his birth-date, while the three ships were either celestial tokens of the three Magi, or simply symbolic of the Trinity itself.

The timing was impeccable. Naturally, hopes and aspirations ran high. The euphoric air of jubilance and rebirth had miraculously quashed the innate fear many would've had otherwise, namely of storm troopers invading with malicious intent. The fact that the aliens had broadcasted their peaceful message of greetings in numerous Earthly languages, well before they exited their ships, also placated the masses, especially those in dire straits and despair, as many were.

In fact, over two-thirds of the world had been mired in a malaise for over four hundred years, a dark and debilitating time that deadened the hearts, minds, and souls of millions. Most had no clue that a Dark Ages had existed long before, or that the Italian Renaissance broke Western civilization out of that quagmire, let alone how the future nations of Spain, Portugal, France, England, Dutch Netherlands, and eventually the United States advanced our portion of the world, as that rich history—and all the disciplines of higher education—had become esoteric knowledge reserved for only a select few. In fact, public libraries had become as scarce as Switchboard Operators—basically, there were none. And so it has remained that way for four hundred years, as millions have lived uneventful and gloomy lives, shackled in poverty and many dying young from malnutrition, depression, or suicide. Therefore, the aliens' arrival had indeed appeared to be one of great hope and salvation.

I, Raul Ortega, had the good fortune of being one of Earth's two spokespeople, being that I was a prominent member of the United Nations, and that my country—a third-world nation in the Western hemisphere and steeped in the New Dark Ages—nicely offset the undisputed world leader, situated in the Eastern hemisphere. That superpower happened to be China, represented by Leann Chung, a fellow UN delegate.

You see, four centuries ago, my nation, the United States, had plummeted to its absolute nadir. It was thrust into its deepest depression in history. Unable to sustain its economic infrastructure, it cracked like a levee, as a deluge of unemployment, crime, drug use, homelessness, and bankruptcies decimated the once rich and prosperous land. Being one of the elite has granted me access to the administration's handful of private libraries. As such, my knowledge of America's glorious past is predicated on my reading of history and the photos and videos that survived, as I've only known the squalor, drudgery, and depravity that have plagued my country. Therefore, I've been very fortunate to have access to a wealth of information about our past. And what I've learned is that the laudable philosophy of being humane and hospitable had unfortunately caused a tsunami of repercussions; a backlash that caught many of our nation's ancestors off guard, as an onslaught of malicious migrants and fallacious refugees from third-world nations saturated the American empire by the millions, far outnumbering the goodhearted and industrious souls who sought asylum or just a better life.

According to surviving statistical accounts, forty-six percent of the nation's citizenry had foreseen this calamity as inevitable, yet numerous politicians and media pundits derided them as xenophobes or racists. In hindsight, we now know that while some indeed were, the vast majority were merely perceptive, not prejudiced. The basic fact that not all humans are benevolent souls with respect for others had become manifest in its most ugly form.

Just as Mohamed Atta could never be a Billy Graham, nor Hitler be a Gandhi, the intrinsic dichotomy of human nature can never be forged into a unified whole of utter peace and harmony, no matter how much we try or pray for such worldly bliss.

From the oral traditions handed down through my family, I was informed—and firmly believe—that the USA was built upon the backs of immigrants of all nations, religions, and ethnicities, which indeed it had been. In fact, that's what made America great. Yet, the error our leaders and many of our distant ancestors made was one not anticipated; namely, a substantial portion of the new wave of illegal foreigners didn't share the same beliefs or social mores. And that influx of fifteen million quickly multiplied to forty million due to their higher reproduction rate, giving them a stronger voice to demand change, as well as being coddled and empowered by very charitable yet beguiled legislators, which inevitably led to America's Fall.

From reading ancient history, I also discovered that the same deadly fall happened to the Roman Empire, when barbarians casually infiltrated their borders, then slowly caused the deterioration of the Romans' superior culture and laws from within. The misleading notion that Rome fell from without, by military invasions, was a misnomer—the internal damage had already been done. Yet, those perfunctory—yet visually shocking—attacks by Attila and Odoacer had perpetuated the fear of foreign invasion upon all future nations, while ignoring the true and most deadly contagion; namely, that of passively welcoming immigrants with aberrant ideologies and hostile intentions.

And so in America, there was a new kind of immigrant; a deadly one, unlike those who had come in goodwill with homogeneous beliefs, such as my Mexican family, or the countless others from various nations who became productive citizens. Our families, in contrast, had come to America not only with hopes of bettering their lives and their children's lives, but also to assimilate into the superior culture that drew them in the first place, knowing that their destination, and new homeland, had clearly proven to be an enhanced society and beacon of hope. Moreover, they had come with an abiding respect for the rule of law and eagerly sought citizenship to become full-fledged Americans, as the pursuit of happiness was there for all.

However, the virulent breed of newcomers had somehow forgotten that they had left their archaic backwater or militantly overrun homelands to seek a better life, and instead unlawfully infiltrated America to wreak havoc or seek entitlements from all that the rich nation had to offer, thereby thrusting all the productive, law-abiding taxpayers into debt. Worse still, they, along with several native factions, made devastating demands, as the accommodating sanctuary even catered to their pleas to strip the nation of its traditional holidays and tear down historic statues that they claimed insulted their heritages, while maliciously castigating the very people who had built the prosperous and highly advanced nation that they enjoyed and lived in and eventually conquered—or rather, destroyed.

Just as a very small faction of radical jihadists in the Middle East managed to overrun the peaceful, moderate Muslims, the miscreants here had likewise prevailed. The ugly cycle of life had played itself out, and the illustrious history and culture of America was erased and replaced, thus it inevitably sank into a cheap replica of the third-world nations and tribes of its new third-world inhabitants. Sadly, the rich fabric of America had been slowly eaten away by an infestation of *Tineola* larvae.

The good news, however, was that the extraterrestrials offered Americans the promise of a rebirth, a Renaissance to escape the New Dark Ages we had long suffered under for four centuries. As noted, I was at the forefront of communicating with the aliens, along with Leann Chung, who, despite being an intelligent woman, naturally tried to hinder my negotiations on behalf of the United States and our few remaining allies. China's cunning hegemonistic plans, during the early 2020s, had eventually paid off, as they had engulfed most of Asia, including Russia, India, both Koreas, Japan, and much of the African continent. World War III hadn't been globally devastating, as many had expected, being that the battle was quick and it didn't involve Western nations.

Meanwhile, the radical Muslims had gained control of the entire Middle East and Northern Africa, and most of Europe, as Germany, France, and England fell under their reign, not by warfare, but from within, as their goodwill towards unregulated and hostile immigrants had likewise caused their own demise. Most of the books of Western scientists, explorers, inventors, artists, writers, composers, and thinkers had been burned, expunged in the Great Purge of 6/6/66.

Even comparable books in America had long been destroyed, not by Sharia law, as had happened in Europe, but by appeasement—caving into the aberrant directives of the truculent factions of rebel rousers, many of whom harbored ancient vendettas against the nation, not realizing that most of their ancestors had committed even more egregious sins, as all races, at one time or another, engaged in bloodletting. The sad fact remains: All nations and tribes were created in blood, not with benevolence.

Meanwhile, both American continents had also been renamed—North Land and South Land, respectively—as not to aggrandize one race or native tribe over another. Even Washington D.C. had been renamed; now simply known as the Capital District.

Furthermore, Lincoln's proposition that "all men are created equal" had been taken literally, and to enforce Honest Abe's axiom, the Equalizer Laws were passed, which denied those with high IQs to be granted scholarships or to attend Ivy League colleges, which were reserved for those with lower GPA's or minority status. Meanwhile, the wages of all U.S. citizens were mandated to be the same $30,000.00 a year salary. So, the hot dog vendor, brain surgeon, professional athlete, social worker, movie star, fast-food server, Wall Street financial advisor, and janitor, for example, all earned equal salaries. The collapse of capitalism—which many Americans had chided for its unwieldy, tyrannical nature—likewise had an adverse effect, which augmented the downfall of the nation. Capitalism, we've learned, was deeply flawed, yet socialism proved deadly. All colleges and most businesses—since our empire's fall in 2066—have evaporated, leaving us in the pathetic state in which we are now ensnared. For four, long centuries, the majority of peoples on the two huge continents have been relegated to living in ramshackle homes or makeshift huts, all without running water or electricity amid mounting squalor and rampant crime.

Nevertheless, the two undisputed world leaders in recent years are the authoritarian Chinese and the Islamic Caliphate, the latter headquartered in what used to be Iran. Borders had since been erased, as the Islamic Empire had become one large expanse after it annihilated Israel in 2063 with a nuclear holocaust, then rendered all the moderate and respectable Muslims in the region into submission. In private, many moderates still chide their overlords, saying the Fertile Crescent had become the new Fanatical Precedent. In their eyes, their future, too, looks terrifyingly bleak.

As such, my appeal to the aliens five years ago had been of the utmost importance; that's if we ever had a chance of resurrecting America and, more importantly, Western civilization itself. As I explained, the aliens had offered the world humble and gracious greetings in numerous languages, which they had broadcasted on every cable TV channel and the Internet, having tapped into our global communication networks.

The three large ships, at first, hovered some five hundred feet above the desert sand in the Yucca Flats of Nevada. That location, I later learned, had been chosen due to its high level of radiation—radiation created by mankind's maniacal, atomic bomb testing back in the latter days of WWII and the subsequent Cold War. Those tests had culminated into over a thousand detonations during the Red Scare, causing massive levels of radiation to seep into the earth, levels that appealed to our alien guests. For, as I also discovered, the aliens not only utilize radiation as fuel, but more importantly, for molecular regeneration and mutation.

When the aliens finally decided to exit their spacecrafts, it was determined that it would only be among my two fellow delegates and myself, for in addition to Leann Chung was the caliph of the Islamic Empire, who had voiced his outrage at being excluded from the initial negotiations. Despite the United States' tenuous relationship with China—which had compounded our Depression, by monopolizing manufacturing and stealing trade secrets—we still maintained open lines of trade with the superpower, even if only as impoverished consumers.

However, the extreme ideological and religious rift between the radical Islamists now in control and the myriad of religions in our land had never been resolved, and unfortunately never will. The polar beliefs of the opposing factions go beyond oil and water, and are more akin to Heaven and Hell, as "never the twain shall meet," which Rudyard Kipling so aptly decreed in his 1889 poem, *The Ballad of East and West.*

As such, that innate animosity still permeates world relations, and having had to welcome the radicalized caliph into our negotiation process with the aliens five years ago was the ultimate test in diplomacy and humility.

Nevertheless, that meeting was a milestone, not only in my humble personal life, but a major event in human history, as three aliens (one from each ship), descended from their glistening, metallic crafts through vertical columns of light, which I presume were energized particle beams. Yet once the three beings materialized on the Nevada desert floor, our six human eyes simultaneously bulged as we indecorously gasped. We had not anticipated their weird physical configurations, having been previously lulled into believing they'd look somewhat humanlike by their linguistic versatility, not to mention their personable charm while we listened to their broadcasts of good faith.

Needless to say, our hearts raced that day as sweat moistened our faces, no doubt by Nevada's intense desert heat, but more so by the hideous creatures that stood before us. Each was comprised of a large and almost parasitic head, with two big eyes, one wrapped around the front of its head, the other around the back, giving it 360 degrees of vision; two octopus-like arms, each outfitted with a series of finger-like extrusions, making them extremely adroit at manipulating objects; and in lieu of legs, featured a large, ball-shaped roller. Half of the roller was exposed, the other half engaged in a huge, hip-like socket, akin to the tracking ball on an old computer mouse, thus enabling the creature to glide easily, precisely, and quickly in any direction. I must admit, despite its unsightly appearance, it's a well-designed organism, highly functional, and very practical in most respects.

Their lead commander, Airam Atnas, had exited from their largest ship, and was flanked by two subordinate officers, one from each of the two smaller ships. The Zoaronians, which they called themselves, were astute enough to know that Earthlings would be fearful of their peculiar looks and had requested that we supply them with DNA samples of three deceased humans. They had mastered the art of molecular generation and informed us that they would transform their bodies into three humanoids, each containing an amalgamation of both the Earthling and Zoaronian specimens. They adamantly stipulated that the human DNA samples contain no known defects, and should be extracted only from our most superior specimens. Naturally, that request in itself caused a great deal of debate among us few Earthlings in the know—those being just twelve high-ranking officials from each of our three representative nations.

The notion of *superior* had different meanings for each of us, and this had caused me great concern, especially regarding the radical Islamists, whose long history of Jihadist massacres of innocent citizens, and the destruction of iconic statues of other religions, posed a moral minefield, not to mention how they initially demanded that the Zoaronians submit to Allah, citing them as infidels. Having evaded that dilemma, we three representative nations had each supplied the Zoaronians with DNA samples: the Chinese had chosen Hun Su, the revered and recently deceased father of the sitting dictator; the Islamists had chosen their previous caliph, Mehdi Mohammad Khomeni, who had been assassinated by moderate rebel Muslims; and my nation returned with the DNA of Albert Einstein, as a sample of his brain tissue had miraculously survived the many centuries of turmoil and degradation of our nation, thanks to the proficiency of the Mütter Museum.

Airam Atnas made the decision that he would acquire the DNA of Einstein, while his second in command, Anin, took on Hun Su's DNA, and the third commander, Atnip, the Islamic caliph's DNA. The miraculous transformations took a week to complete, and when the aliens emerged from their spacecrafts, the results were stunning, yet somewhat varied.

I had anticipated seeing a complete recreation of Albert Einstein, but what appeared before me had only some physical characteristics of the great physicist: the wild gray hair and bushy mustache being the most prominent. Yet the other distinct features of the great man were indeed there, as were the features of each of the two other humanoid-alien hybrids. As for cognitive abilities, each new specimen exhibited varying degrees of their human subject's character, yet the Zoaronians' superior brains governed most thought and speech processes.

Airam and I had bonded rather quickly that day, and I had even invited him to my Manhattan bachelor pad on the Upper East Side. We had spoken briefly and, unexpectedly, he invited me into his highly polished spacecraft, which was parked in the large vacant lot where Madison Square Garden once stood. The ship was immense and impressive, being a huge chromium orb with gargantuan spikes radiating out of it, along with a rear propulsion appendage. The interior was likewise a vision to behold. Having lived my whole life in a broken-down nation, amid the dismal eyesores of decrepit buildings, it was truly a feast for the eyes to see the posh interior of his ship and its sophisticated operating systems. Airam had given me a brief tour; then, with the blink of his telekinetic eye, the ship transported us from New York to Monument Valley, on the border of Arizona and Utah. That we had traveled that great distance in literally one second, without whiplash of any kind, was also a most peculiar but exhilarating experience.

We exited the ship that day and peered around us. Contentedly, Airam gazed at the towering, red mountains and large rocks with their irregular configurations. He admired the raw and serene beauty of Earth's natural terrain, but made one thing quite clear. He was displeased with mankind's "ruination of a nation," as he put it. Urban areas, he thought, were hideous eyesores. And indeed they were, since all that remained since the fall were run-down buildings, many of which were reduced to ruinous skeletons where drug dealers thrived, while piles of debris and human waste littered most streets and alleys. The images of old New York, and other cities I had seen in books, were just that, old memories of what used to be. The handful of old buildings that remained included the Empire State Building, which was our most enduring symbol of the glory of our distant past. Yet, it, too, was in need of repair.

Nevertheless, as we stood in the rocky desert, our conversations explored a plethora of subjects, and it was clear that Airam was genuinely interested in our species.

With mixed feelings, I had cautiously questioned him: "I'm glad you like our planet's natural beauties, Airam. But I must ask you, *why*? And, *why* do you have this fascination with *us*?"

His response had been a welcome sign, as he replied, "Mr. Ortega, our interest in your species and planet is not for conquest but for exploration and research. Although our race is vastly superior, we have learned long ago that much can be gleaned from all things in nature, be they sophisticated—such as your most complex computers—or simplistic—as a rock, for example." His eyes scanned the terrain. "Which just might contain uranium."

His last response had caused me some concern, as doubts had always hovered underneath our warm exchanges. Yet I tackled the situation head-on when I replied, "Airam, many of our people have serious concerns about your intentions. Your initial landing had many Christians hailing you as messengers of God, here to announce the arrival of their Savior, Jesus Christ. You see, His long-awaited return had been prophesied by the Lord Himself, thousands of years ago." As he listened intently, I continued, "Billions have lived and died over the centuries in despair at the Lord's failure to return. So, you see, your arrival has raised the hopes of millions. But now that your alien origins have been revealed, they've not only lost hope, but are frightened."

Airam scratched his bushy, Einstein-like mustache as he glanced down at the reddish dirt and tapped it with his foot, as if analyzing it. His eyes veered up toward the heavens, then down at mine with profound gravity. "Mr. Ortega, Earthlings have rallied behind many different gods over the course of countless centuries, each somewhat unique, yet all sharing very similar traits. I have learned that your people have worshipped Ra, Horus, Apollo, Zeus, Mithras, Hashem, Jesus, Allah, Buddha and countless others. Quite obviously, they can't *all* be gods, now can they?"

Before I could answer, he continued, "Therefore, except for *one*, all the rest must be false gods." A haughty smile came over his face. "Or perhaps, mankind has it all wrong, Raul, and *all* of them are fabrications." As I listened with growing curiosity, he went on, "Furthermore, don't you find it curious how all of those alleged gods only originated in specific locations, among select races? Why would the *one-and-only* true God appear to only a distinct few—in your case, only to tan Middle Easterners and a handful of white Romans? Why wasn't Jesus Chinese? Or African? Or why wouldn't your one God visit *all* of His children, if in fact they all *were* His children? Or why are all these current gods men? Why not women? Or something else entirely?"

As I explained to Airam that day, I didn't know. That was beyond my comprehension. I informed him that it was often said that the Lord works in mysterious ways. His response startled me.

"If that's the case, Mr. Ortega, I could very easily persuade *all* Earthlings that *I'm* the one and only true God, simply by displaying my ominous powers. Or, as your scriptures say, punish them with brimstone and fire, for they have all worshipped false gods."

A disturbing shiver ran down my spine that day as I responded, "Airam, it's quite clear that humans are no match for your race's superior intellect. But I truly hope that along with your impressive acquisition of knowledge you also developed a genuine sense of compassion and benevolence, and that such rhetoric is purely hypothetical."

Airam unexpectedly chuckled as he peered into the distance at the intriguing formations of Monument Valley. As I stood in the desert, nervously awaiting his response, he continued to scan and admire the alien-like horizon, which perhaps looked like his home planet, when finally, he said, without looking at me, "Yes, Raul. I assure you, it was only as you say, purely hypothetical."

He then pulled a briar pipe out of his pocket and lit it up. He took a few puffs, then turned toward me as the aromatic tobacco spiraled upward. "I'll have you know something else, Raul. My analysis of all your manmade gods had come, in large part," he tapped his cranium, "from my other self: namely, Einstein's formidable brain; formidable, at least for a human, that is."

I was taken aback by that response. "So, you really *are* part Einstein?"

He smiled. "Of course, Raul. Did you think our expertise at hybrid mutations was faulty or a farce, like your worship in false gods?"

I smirked. "Let's leave God out of this, but I see you smoke Albert's pipe, as well."

He shrugged. "What can I say? I like—or rather, *he* likes—the tactile feel of a pipe. That is, when it's clenched between his teeth." He shifted the pipe from one side of his mouth to the other, lightly chewed on it, then extracted it. He gazed down at the brown piece of shiny wood as its smoldering tobacco rose up into his eyes. He blinked. "It's actually not too bad. The feel between the teeth, that is." He rubbed his watery eyes, then his chest, and coughed. "Though I'm not too enamored with the irrational process of inhaling smoke, Mr. Ortega, flavored or not."

In hindsight, I recall vividly that moment in the Arizona wilderness, when I'd had enough of small talk about pipes and smoking, and got back on track, as I asked him, pointedly: *"Why,* Airam? And I'm not asking Einstein, I'm asking *you.* Why did you choose planet Earth? And, *how* did you find us? After all, our blue and green pebble is just an insignificant dot amid a vast universe of infinite space."

The corners of Airam's Einsteinian mustache had risen to reveal a sagacious smile, as he said, "Raul, we on planet Zoaron have what you call astronomers, too. Yet they and their equipment are far more advanced. As you know, the stars you see in your sky are visual illusions—*ghosts,* if you will, of the original suns or planets that radiated that light thousands, millions, or even billions of years ago. That light traversed the universe to reach your eyes, some of which represent stars that still exist, while others are from stars that were obliterated by massive collisions or supernovas and have long-since died. As I said—ghosts, illusions. Yet those reflections live on for all eternity."

I recall how that last comment, *'reflections live on for all eternity,'* had intrigued me that day, as he pointed to his shiny, chrome spaceship and we reentered the craft. As we took a seat around a large table, made of some unknown alloy, Airam continued, "To help you understand this concept more clearly, Mr. Ortega, those images are like your motion pictures, keeping a record of all that has transpired, from the star's birth to its death. And your planet's full history continues to radiate out into the universe, at all angles, just as the sun reflects your image to everyone's eyes around you in *all* directions—left, right, top, bottom, and every minuscule increment in between. You see, your reflections and actions, including your speech, are broadcast in all dimensions, not just through a single lens, like your movies. As such, Earth's history and its trillions of humans, from prehistoric days until now, have been projected out into the universe in a starburst-like radiance. So, you see, our astronomers had received your planet's emissions over a long period of time. Better still, we discovered a way to accelerate those light and sound waves, thus compiling millions of years of data in only four years' time."

Airam's startling revelation had struck me like a lightning bolt. He and his race had not only received and recorded millions of years of Earth's visual reflections, but also its audio transmissions—a premise that seemed to be glaringly implausible. I looked at his Einstein-esque face as if he had two alien heads, as I replied, "Airam, it's common knowledge that light and sound waves ultimately dissipate. I'm no scientist, but I know that breaks the laws of physics. It just can't be."

Meanwhile, Airam had spotted an ant. The tiny critter had managed to gain access to his craft, and it crawled on the table, attempting to eat some type of biscuit the aliens ate. Airam placed his finger before the ant, which crawled on his hand. He then raised his hand toward me. There was an odd glint in his alien eyes as he glanced at the ant, then at me. "Mr. Ortega, one of the major follies of the human race is that they often think only within the confines of their own limited minds." Airam then petted the ant's little head.

I received his innuendo loud and clear, as I said with a smirk, "There's no need to be rude, Airam. I know we humans are no match for your superior intellects, but an *ant*? Really?"

Airam chuckled. "I tease…it was only a jest, as you say." He gingerly placed the ant down, without crushing it—which I took as a good sign. He then continued, "Just because human eyes and ears observe the dissipation of light and sound waves does not mean that others with advanced capabilities can't observe what lies beyond your limited means. Or in your terms, think of how a dog can hear higher frequencies than humans, or how an eagle can see farther and clearer. Better yet, think of how galaxy collisions, gamma-ray bursts, and other cosmic phenomena occur at wavelengths beyond the range of human vision, and can only be seen via the use of special instruments." With his telekinetic powers, Airam activated a hologram that appeared on the table before us. Suddenly, a series of fascinating gamma rays materialized in a visual form that my deficient eyes could now detect.

"In essence, Mr. Ortega, don't dispel what your human senses are incapable of processing. For even I…" he paused and rubbed his temple, then smiled. "Or rather, *Einstein*, knew to dispel what had been common knowledge or that which was *assumed* by others, for in so doing, he, or *we*," he chuckled, "posited the brilliant theory that light can indeed bend." He closed his eyes and rubbed his temples harder, as if subduing the conflicting brainwaves of his human half, then opened his eyes. "As you may know, Raul, that theory was later proven to be true by Sir Arthur

Eddington in 1919. What became known as gravitational lensing had become an important tool in astrophysics, which simultaneously confirmed my—or rather *Einstein's*—radical theory of relativity as being quite accurate."

Those powerful words that day—from this Einsteinian-alien—had given me serious and profound pause for thought, as did his astounding revelation about their audio-visual recordings of Earth. Airam proceeded to explain that planet Zoaron was in a somewhat fixed location, which meant that the Earth's rotations only transmitted its daytime activities to his planet. As such, they had recorded trillions of hours of diverse footage and conversations by countless people of Earth's past. Their sophisticated computers churned day and night for four years to separate and catalogue the more productive people from the indolent masses, and the results were mind-boggling.

Once again, Airam glanced at the table and activated another hologram. Astounded, I watched actual footage of Moses, Anaximander, Plato, Augustus Caesar, Confucius, Mohammad, Da Vinci, Queen Elizabeth, George Washington, Harriet Tubman, Marie Curie, Gandhi, Enrico Fermi, Franklin and Eleanor Roosevelt, Nikola Tesla, Margaret Thatcher, Steve Jobs, and countless others. These titans of the past were all brought before my very eyes and ears, as I watched not documentaries with fictitious actors, but the real, living and breathing people captured in the course of their amazing lives.

The aliens' sophisticated audio-visual recorder had the capacity to pinpoint and enlarge specific areas of the planet, as if a powerful astro-video camera with an ultra-sensitive microphone, thus being able to concentrate on certain individuals, as the aforementioned names attest. I was truly thunderstruck; the immense value that this one technological advancement would have for the human race seemed incalculable. To be able to study heroes of our past first-hand and learn their *true* actions, not those penned into history by fallible third-party scribes or biased cronies, would be a great tool and awakening, one that could very well fuel another Renaissance. One very much needed.

Yet, as I stated, that was five years ago, when the aliens had first landed. Over the course of those five years, tensions had become strained, as Anin, who had taken on Hun Su's DNA, and Atnip, the hybrid who contained the Islamic caliph's DNA, had gotten into violent disputes over world control. Anin fostered China's expansionist agenda, while Atnip led jihadist raids into Chinese territories. It was clear that the humanoid aspects of both of their constitutions were exerting greater mind control over their alien selves and exacerbating the inherent problems of the human race.

Meanwhile, Airam's advanced mind, aided by Einstein's powerful logic, had unfortunately failed to coax his subordinates into a truce. Last year, another World War—this one labeled WWIV—erupted between the two belligerents. That clash came as a great disappointment, for the United States had made miraculous progress over the first four years under Airam's council, which gave rise to a glorious rebirth. The masses had been reeducated and energized with a patriotic sense of pride that united the once polarized populace. Working in unison, the nation had reinvented itself and was showing signs of great promise.

However, WWIV had proved disastrous, as the destructive hands of war even inflicted hammering blows to North Land—recently renamed North America—despite our neutrality. To our horror, the global conflict had escalated, turning much of the world into a raging inferno. That's when Airam lost faith in his human subjects—who, he had said, succumbed to their base instincts, some borne out of greed, others out of religious fanaticism.

Viewing the human race as a lost cause, Airam chose to flee the insanity, akin to how his other self had fled Nazi Germany in his time. As such, he had turned away in disgust on that tragic day, entered his ship, and sailed for home.

Meanwhile, the two warring nations had ravaged large swatches of Earth, as nuclear and conventional weapons razed cities across the globe, including those in the USA. Boston, Chicago, the Capital District, and New York City were turned into ruins by Atnip and the Islamic Empire, citing our neutrality as evidence of being infidels who failed to defend Allah.

Worse yet, although the radical Muslims had lost their Middle Eastern territories in the aftermath to Atnip and the Chinese Empire, they subjugated the entire North American continent and much of South Land over the past year to their ideological will, and had relocated their capital city to New York, now called New Tehran.

Atnip had erected an entirely new city and covered it with an enormous glass dome, which was both climate-controlled and impervious to most conventional weapons. By decree, only Muslims were permitted within the domed city's sacred glass walls, and to this very day, many courageous American rebels still lurk outside in the ruins of old New York City, myself included. Night and day, brazen rebels carry out guerilla attacks on the occupiers, and have even hung American flags out the windows of burnt-out buildings in sheer defiance. While others, under my direction, have been supplied with far greater resources than rifles and knives—namely with antiquated, but quite effective, twentieth-century stealth fighters and four old nuclear warheads, which had been long forgotten and stored in bunkers under the Nevada desert.

In fact, they recently secured our first great victory at dawn today, by shooting down Atnip's coveted spacecraft, which now sits in New York harbor, looking like a defunct satellite amid the ruins of the old city, as the Empire State Building—our cherished symbol—sits decrepitly nearby, looking like a sinking ship. Yet, within the shiny exterior of Atnip's chrome spaceship, I see reflections of conquest. For, as I speak, another squadron of heavily equipped stealth bombers are making their way to penetrate the great dome of New Tehran.

Amid the adrenaline rushes of anticipation, another revelation just dawned on me: I now realize that Anin, when reversed, is Nina. While Atnip is Pinta, and Airam Atnas is Santa Maria. Our three alien explorers had taken on the names of three vessels that changed the world as we knew it. And whether by design or coincidence, Airam was indeed like Columbus, who had left the New World disgusted and forlorn to return home, while his subordinates remained to cause much havoc amid the miraculous advances that would eventually spawn the greatest country the world had ever known, a super civilization, the likes of which had never been seen before on Earth: namely, the United States of America.

It is with the greatest hopes that, after this war, the country will reign supreme once again, as the maddening cycles of war and peace, or thriving empire and squalid backwater, are all a part of humankind's flawed DNA. Conceding to that sad fact, I now take solace in knowing that our New Dark Ages are nearing an end, and better days most surely lie ahead. For the revelation is now manifest: those with integrity of heart and unyielding resolve must always fight to attain or regain the splendors of human ingenuity, tolerance, and freedom from the recurring tides of malevolent forces that wish to wash them all away.

With my rifle in hand, I stand ready, behind the ruins of the New York Life Insurance Building with my platoon sitting at my side, while stealth fighters whiz over our heads.

Frank Marino, Bob Johnson, and Jessica Mills, my steadfast lead rebels, look at me with anticipation, as Jessica says, "This could be it!" While Frank corrects, "This *is* it, Jess! They *must* score, or game over!"

These three leaders each have beautiful families, as do all of the men and women in our platoon, each knowing full well what's at stake in the next few minutes or days.

As we firmly grip our weapons and peer nervously up at our attack force, we suddenly hear enemy surface-to-air missiles scream into the sky. With our hearts in our mouths, we watch with bated breath as the missiles spiral upward and chase after our fighters. To our eternal delight, they miss their evasive targets, as the stealth fighters swoop down and fire upon the colossal glass dome.

Bob, Frank, and Jessica lean forward, their eyes fixed on the fighters' sidewinders, while others swallow hard and cross their fingers.

"Have confidence, Patriots," I say. "Those pilots are the best."

With consecutive shots, the first three missiles strike the dome, as fireballs of raw light and black smoke erupt. In unison, several Patriots belt out rebel yells!

However, as the smoke dissipates, we notice that the explosions only caused minor blemishes to the seemingly impenetrable dome. As hearts begin to sink, I declare with conviction, "Don't lose faith, troops. I supplied those fighters with a helluva lot more firepower than that."

No sooner do I speak, than the ground quakes violently and the sky explodes! Four direct hits pierce the dome, causing it to crack and shatter!

In awe, we watch as the blinding light and heat assaults our bodies, while, in the distance, massive chunks of glass rain down upon the Islamic citadel. Peering through my binoculars, I see enemy troops being crushed under the falling debris, while others scatter aimlessly in panic amid the harrowing destruction and mounting chaos.

Although my dreaded enemy, to see humans dying amid such a hellish cauldron of fire and brutal carnage saddens my soul. War truly is the definition of insanity. Taking a deep breath, I purge the tragic folly of humankind, with its eternal cycles of violence and victory, and I engage the moment, for our time is upon us, and if the ugly game of war allows only one winner, that winner must be us, those committed to freedom, tolerance, and humanity.

As more fiery blasts illuminate our faces and very souls, as if the sun itself were before us, my heart pounds to the challenge with resolve. With pride surging through our veins, we rise to our feet and cock our weapons.

Now consumed with glorious visions of a New Renaissance, I peer at my compatriots and yell, "Let's go, Patriots. The future is in our hands. *Charge!*"

Meanwhile, all around me, I hear the glorious refrain: "*Viva* USA!"

THE GORGON

Valery Casella excitedly stuffed one suitcase with her clothes, then another with a variety of odd lab samples, as she envisioned her new adventure in Japan—one she and her parents were about to embark on for three months over summer vacation.

Meanwhile, her father stood in the foyer and tapped his foot impatiently on the decorative marble floor. He glanced at the time on his cell phone, then at his wife, Angela. With a smirk, he rolled his eyes toward Valery, who finally exited her bedroom at the end of the hallway. "Would you look at her! She moves like a ninety-year old invalid."

As Angela giggled, Peter gazed back at his daughter. "Hurry up, Valery! The limo has been here for fifteen minutes already—*waiting*...waiting for *you!*"

"Don't worry, Dad," Valery said calmly, not even looking up as she refastened her partially zipped backpack. "I'm ready. You worry too much. Take a chill pill."

Peter's lips twisted. "Listen, sweetheart, once you get into college you'll find out that your science professors will not appreciate your tardiness. They have little sympathy for AP students who accelerate out of high school, especially those who act in line with their age rather than their intelligence. And that even goes for fifteen-year old savants, like *you!*"

"Don't worry, Pops. I have the whole summer to mature before I go to Johns Hopkins for Evolutionary Biology."

Peter rolled his eyes. "Yes, three months in Japan will somehow transform you from a carefree child into an adult." He shook his head. "And dear Lord, Evolutionary Biology? Why you chose not to apply that brilliant brain of yours to a profession where you can one day make millions, rather than sitting in some remote laboratory making peanuts, is beyond me."

"Yes, Father," she said as she walked toward him, "higher learning for truly worthy causes *is* beyond you."

Peter would have snapped back at her, but her endearing smile laced with a tinge of sarcasm was too precious for him not to chuckle. Especially since Valery had awed him ever since she was a little girl. It hadn't taken very long for him to realize that all of their study sessions throughout grade school had soon turned him into a dinosaur, while Valery evolved into a mini Madame Curie. And that her abnormal brain seemed to gravitate toward Evolutionary Biology and Microbiology was something he could never seem to change.

Valery's sophisticated home laboratory and experiments in trying to produce hybrids of various animals not only impressed her high school science teachers, but also the college scouts from Harvard, Stanford, and Johns Hopkins who had visited them, each eager to snatch the wunderkind up to enhance his or her own college's reputation. How much they really cared about such kids' future careers was an unknown variable, but the bottom line was that Valery was a gifted girl, and Peter knew that somehow she was right. Higher learning for scientists was an extremely small niche market for an elite class of world thinkers, those who dedicated their lives not to the mighty dollar but to the Promethean task of trying to invent or discover things that would enhance humanity, knowing full well such breakthroughs only came to a small fraction of their esteemed colleagues. While the ignorant masses showered athletes with scholarships, adulation, and multi-million-dollar contracts to play games, Valery knew the people who truly made the earth-shattering changes to humankind were the unsung heroes making average wages in the remote shadows.

Peter smiled. "Okay, sweetheart. You're right, I *don't* fully understand, because I was raised to make money." As she hugged him and looked up into his loving eyes, he reiterated one of his poignant lectures. "As you know, sweetie, my parents lived through the Depression. They felt firsthand the fear of worrying about where their next meal would come from, or *if* they'd ever eat again. Therefore, many of those who survived vowed never to be without money again. So they horded cash, became spend-thrifts, and instilled in their children the importance of making money, as that was the only solution to putting food on the table, clothes on their backs, a roof over their heads, and bettering their lives. And I became a CPA and business consultant because of their legitimate fears and concerns. And while I agree that my job is truly menial compared to a scientist's, I do put food on the table, clothes on your back, and a nice, big roof over your lovely little head."

Valery glanced up at the cathedral ceiling, envisioning the massive roof that, indeed, covered the ten thousand square foot mansion her father gifted them all with. Her head lowered, ashamed, as she stepped back. "I'm sorry, Dad. I didn't mean to be rude. It's just that I—"

"I know, sweetheart, I know," Peter said, knowing that Valery was certainly smart enough to recognize the injustices and ignorance that plagued society, which would further prohibit her from making the kind of money that movie stars and athletes made—or even what *he* made, unless, of course, she was one of those lucky savants who made a major breakthrough. But the odds of that were like coming home from Vegas three times in a row, each time a huge winner. Sure, it happens to some, but only *some*. As a father, all Peter wished for was for Valery to be able to survive any obstacle life threw at her, and hopefully surpass his good fortune to climb several steps higher on the proverbial ladder of success. But being an Evolutionary Biologist didn't seem a route that would garner the financial rewards or recognition that would warrant the lifelong dedication and sacrifices it required.

"Let's just get our bags into the limo," Peter said as he glanced nervously at the time again.

Catching their Delta flight to Tokyo, the Casellas landed at Haneda Airport and were greeted by Riku Hataki and his eighteen-year old daughter, Sakura, who wore a posh designer dress and a decorative Hermès scarf around her head.

"Ah, Peter! So good to see you," Riku said as he eagerly grasped his hand and shook it vigorously to emphasize his awareness of American customs. "Seeing you in the flesh is much better than through Skype, yes?"

Peter smiled. "Yes, Riku, it is. And thank you for taking us into your home. That wasn't necessary, but very kind and generous. We're truly honored."

Riku nodded in Japanese fashion. "No, no, the honor is all mine, Peter. We at Toyota expect good things from you. The recalls have been quite damaging to our bottom line over the past several years, and we need the keen eye and sharp pencil of someone like you to help us get back on track."

"Well, no promises, but I'll certainly try my best."

Peter pivoted around. "Allow me to introduce my wife, Angela, and my daughter, Valery."

As they stepped forward, Riku bowed. "It's an honor." He then grasped his daughter's hand and edged her forward, yet his amicable face twitched with a glint of sadness. "This is my daughter, Sakura."

The Casellas all noticed Riku's expression as they each bowed slightly, while questions ran through their minds: *Had Sakura dishonored Riku in some fashion? Was she pregnant and unwed? Did she disobey some Japanese tradition that embarrassed Riku?*

Before they could process it further, Riku pointed and said, "Please, come this way. My chauffer awaits us."

Akito was waiting for them by the stretch, Rolls Royce limo in his black uniform and cap, looking like Bruce Lee as Kato from *The Green Hornet*. He dutifully grasped their luggage and placed it in the trunk, then opened the mid-section doors to escort the three ladies into the limo's central compartment.

Meanwhile, Riku opened the limo's back door, and he and Peter sat in the posh rear section. It was divided by a half-wall and soundproof window, which Riku opened. He then pressed another button, closing the window to Akito's front cab. As the limo began to move forward, he announced, "May I have all your attention?"

As the three ladies turned and faced Riku, he continued, "Before we arrive at my villa, I wish to lay bare some personal information about my family, as transparency eliminates false assumptions and unwarranted concerns. Your comfort, in mind and body, is paramount." He pressed a button and a nicely stocked mini-bar slid out. "First, may I get any of you a drink?"

As Peter and Angela received mixed drinks and the two girls sodas, Riku closed the bar and continued, "We Japanese, by and large, are private people. We keep our burdens to ourselves. That, however, is an old Japanese trait, one that has been deeply ingrained in us, well before America's mighty, liberal influence took hold of our great nation." As the limo headed for the Haneda Airport's exit, Riku mindfully looked out the window. "Do you see this sprawling airfield? Your general, Douglas MacArthur, expanded it in September of 1945, just a month after your nation bombed Hiroshima and Nagasaki and we surrendered."

As the Casellas each shifted uncomfortably in their seats, not knowing where Riku's oration was heading, their host continued, "MacArthur had evicted three thousand families to make room for this magnificent enterprise, which allowed us to build an international airport, one that not only continues to serve millions of people, but was one of many enhancements that enabled Japan to become a productive nation, one dedicated to modernization and innovation, rather than imperial conquest, dictatorship, and destruction." He glanced at each of the Casellas' faces, having recognized their previous trepidations. "Yes, have no fear, I am not one of the select few who still harbor animosity toward your country."

As Angela and Valery sighed with relief, Peter said, "Well, that's comforting to hear, Riku, because I have mixed feelings about what our country did. I know dropping the atomic bombs were necessary to end the war, and oddly enough, did save the lives of countless American and Japanese soldiers, who would have fought a bitter battle otherwise. However, the advent of atomic energy unleashed not just an ominous weapon, but also highly dangerous side effects. And if it's not controlled by rational beings, it could destroy the entire planet. As you know, Riku, many scientists back then feared that mankind had opened Pandora's Box."

Riku's plump cheeks wilted. "Yes, Peter. That brings me to what I would like to impart to all of you." As the limo left the airport and headed to the suburbs of Tokyo, he glanced at his daughter. "Nuclear energy has had a devastating effect on my family. And to avoid any discomfort between us, while you stay with us for the summer, I wish to reveal some unpleasant events that my family has endured. Not to appeal for sympathy, mind you, but rather to simply clear the air, as life will, as it often does, take its own course, many times veering out of our control."

Riku reached over and pressed a button on the console, which opened a panel, revealing a photo of an attractive woman. "That was my darling wife, Koharu," he said as a lump constricted his throat. "She passed away…just last month."

The Casellas each promptly offered their condolences, as Riku waved his hand. "Thank you. But as I said, some things are out of our hands." As the limo continued to drive along scenic side roads, Riku went on. "You see, Koharu was a Nuclear Physicist. She worked at the Fukushima power plant, and was there when the earthquake and tsunami hit. As you know, it caused the terrible meltdown. However, it also triggered a thirty-kilometer evacuation around the contaminated site. Koharu knew she had been exposed to far too much radiation to survive, so she dedicated her declining years to trying to contain and rebuild the plant…right up un…til—" Riku choked up. "Last m-month."

As an uncomfortable silence gripped everyone in the limo, Valery leaned forward and uttered, "Well, Mr. Hataki, I, for one, admire her strong will." As all eyes turned toward the youngest among them, Valery continued, "Koharu chose not to die moaning in self pity. No. Instead, she did something meaningful with her last years on Earth to help others." She offered Riku a sympathetic smile. "You must be very proud?"

Riku's smile managed to slice through the sorrow as he nodded appreciatively. "I thank you, young Miss Casella. Yes, I am most proud, yet also most heartbroken. You see, my lovely Koharu withered before my eyes. That is something no person should ever have to endure. The once vibrant and beautiful love of my life had transformed into a frail skeleton. And to spare us the torture of seeing her decompose, Koharu courageously snuck out in the middle of the night and marched into the ethereal mists of *Aokigahara*."

Valery squinted. "What's *Aokigahara*?"

Riku reopened the bar and refilled his glass with gin and tonic. "Translated, it means the Sea of Trees," he said somberly. Meanwhile, the limo took a hard turn and headed up the mountain toward Hataki's elaborate estate. Riku took a swig, then continued to explain: "*Aokigahara*, Valery, is a sprawling forest on the northwest side of Mount Fuji. It has long been a mysterious place where many go to die. In 2003, over a hundred bodies of people who had committed suicide were found there." He took another swig, and swallowed the potent tonic. "And that's only the ones who were found." He wiped his mouth with his now trembling hand. "Furthermore, the forest is haunted. Not only by *yūrei*, what you call ghosts, but even more frightfully by the dreaded *Gorgon*."

Valery sat upright. "The *Gorgon*? What's that?"

Sakura finally broke her silence. "Father, *stop*! Stop telling them about these foolish myths. There is no such thing as a *Gorgon*." She looked at her father and ripped the decorative scarf off her head, revealing a bald scalp. As the Casellas stifled a gasp, she stridently continued, "He's afraid that I, too, will wander into the forest and be eaten by the *Gorgon*."

Riku fought to contain the tear that threatened to embarrass him, yet failed, as a rivulet streamed down his face. Wiping it away, he replied, "Sakura, my love, I have suffered the agony of watching your mother slowly die, and *yes*, I do believe she was eaten by the *Gorgon*. But I also refuse to see you give up hope!"

"You took me to all the best doctors money could buy, Father," Sakura said with conviction, "and none of them said I have even the slightest chance to survive. The best estimate was two months. Two stinking months!" She looked at Valery. "That's even *before* you leave to go back home! So, I'm sorry that you came all the way to Japan just to hear our family's tragedy and to attend my funeral."

Riku's demeanor rose from that of a private to a general, as he demanded, "Silence! Stop that defeatist talk! You *can* overcome this, Sakura. You *must*!"

As the limo came to a halt in the huge, circular driveway, Sakura opened the door. "Is that an order, Father? As you said, there are things we cannot control. And my life is one of them!" With that, she stepped out of the limo and stormed into the mansion.

Left sitting in the Rolls Royce in awkward silence, the four passengers each glanced at one another, then aimlessly elsewhere, desperately seeking comfort.

The moment was broken when Akito opened the rear door, oblivious to their discussion. "Welcome to the Hataki estate!" he said with a smile.

The Casellas awkwardly forced smiles on their faces, while Riku stepped out, then extended a hand to help the women out of the limo. As Angela and Valery stepped out, he said, "I apologize. I didn't anticipate this getting so emotional."

Angela shook her head sympathetically. "Please, don't apologize, Riku. If you *didn't* get emotional over what you're going through, *that* would have been inexcusable."

As the three adults chatted in the driveway and Akito hauled their luggage into the mansion, Valery darted inside and came up alongside Sakura. "Hey, I'm so sorry to hear..." she paused, then added, "I guess you're sick of hearing that." Her head lowered. "I apologize. I mean... I don't know what to say."

Sakura's dour face actually cracked a semblance of a smile, one that hadn't graced her pretty young face in over a year. "Yes, it's truly depressing, you have no idea." She turned and entered her spacious bedroom, motioning with a slight twitch of her baldhead for Valery to follow.

As Valery stepped in, her eyes lit up. "Wow! I thought *my* bedroom was big, but this is crazy." Her eyes scanned the huge canopy bed draped with silk curtains, then over at the pool table in the far corner, the string of full-sized arcade games with their lights flashing, and a huge vanity made from a rare Toyota GT-One racecar that was cut in half, forming a profile view of the car with the windows being the mirrors, where Sakura could apply her makeup and brush her long, black hair, the latter having vaporized into a depressing memory.

As Sakura sat and stared at the bald, pale figure in the mirror before her, all she could see was the disturbing visage of her dying mother. She ran her palm over her bald scalp. "That's why I want to join my mother, Valery." Her eyes drifted up to Valery's reflection in the mirror. "There's nothing left for me here. I'm a walking ghost, a *yūrei*. I just want to be with my mother, so we can walk together again—in peace, without pain. And without having to see the pain we cause on people's faces, like your family's. But especially my father's. He's suffered enough."

"I suppose I can understand that," Valery muttered. "It's kind of hard to wrap my head around all of this. It's a lot to take in." She gazed aimlessly into a dark, depressing void, a world light-years away from the bubbly, carefree life she had back home. She peered at Sakura. "And it all came so fast. I mean, we just landed here. I never expected...*this*."

"Neither did I," Sakura said as her fingers tepidly tapped her jewelry box. "When the doctor's told me, I turned white, like a *geisha*. But this *geisha* has no desire to entertain with song and dance...unless, perhaps, it's a macabre death dance."

Valery's heart was in her mouth, and her face clearly projected it.

Sakura swiveled around and looked directly at her. "Don't feel sorry, Val. I lost the tears many months ago. They're of no use now. What will be will be. It's out of everyone's control." She spun around again and looked at her pale face in the mirror, then up at Valery's reflection. "That's the worst part of it. The doctors are helpless. My father, with all his millions, is helpless. And I'm helpless, helpless to do anything to rid me of this cancer. This vile intruder that entered my body will never leave, *never*. Not until I'm dead." Again, she stared at herself in the mirror. "That's why I don't even care if the *Gorgon* does exist. Let the ugly beast eat me, and my cancer."

Valery sat down on the chair beside her. "What exactly *is* this *Gorgon*?"

Sakura snickered as she continued to stare at herself in the mirror. "It's some stupid myth that superstitious fools conjured up." Her eyes drifted toward Valery's reflection. "Do you believe in Big Foot or the Loch Ness monster?"

Valery shook her head, as Sakura continued, "Neither do I. And this *Gorgon* is like Scotland's Nessy or your American Big Foot, except it's supposed to be enormous. It's just the wild imagination of silly people." She opened her vanity drawer and pulled out an old newspaper clipping. It featured an imagined rendition of the alleged creature and an article about three witnesses who claimed to see the beast. As Valery gazed at the article, Sakura sniggered. "Supposedly it was either a mad scientist's experiment that went wrong or some mutation from the Fukushima meltdown. Either way, it fled to *Aokigahara* to hide and devour those seeking death, be they suicidal, or those like my mother and myself, who merely seek the mercy of euthanasia."

Valery had already perused the article, which was more of a silly tabloid than informative journalism, and stood up. She paced the room as her mind churned and her hand rubbed her chin. "What does this legendary beast *really* look like? And does it kill for the merciful aspect of death, or for survival?"

Sakura picked up a pad, dabbed it in rouge powder, and patted her alabaster face. "It's said that the *Gorgon* has some intelligence, being partially humanoid, but has the hideous attributes of an ox, warthog, dragon, and vulture, with sharp talons protruding out of all parts of its body in weird places." She picked up an eyeliner pencil and started to pencil-in her missing eyebrows, as she looked up at Valery's reflection. "As for its intentions, what can I say? Many believe it eats people for the fun of it, being a sadistic creature that finds joy in masticating its victims." She placed the pencil down as a solemn expression marred her face. She stared at herself, with her half-finished eyebrows, as she uttered with a quiver, "M-meanwhile, others s-say that after it eats its prey, it howls—or rather, *laughs*, with a bone-chilling squeal that echoes throughout the forest."

Valery chewed her lower lip as she stopped pacing and stared into space. "Jesus! That's creepy." As she thought about it, however, horror soon turned into intrigue.

For several years, Valery had been trying to breed hybrids, and whether this *Gorgon* existed or not, just the idea of it being comprised of multiple breeds fired her imagination and inspiration to continue her research.

She pivoted around and looked at Sakura. "You *can't* go into the Sea of Trees, Sakura. Your father is right. Myth or no myth, that's just a dead end. Why don't you help me instead? Make your last days count. Be useful, like your mother was at Fukushima?"

Sakura squinted, her mind now jolted out of her own misery. "Help *you*?" She wasn't sure if it was a callous insult, or a logical request.

Valery stepped closer. "Yes. I've been working on a radically new process of creating hybrids, and even a potential cure for cancer, among other things, and could use your help."

Sakura rolled her eyes and gazed down at the floor. "I heard you were some whiz-kid prodigy, or something, but—" she looked up at Valery's reflection. "You can't create anything new or come up with a cure for cancer in two months. So, why should I waste my time?"

Valery irritably put her hands on her hips. "Listen, Sakura, try to look beyond your own face in the mirror!" As Sakura recoiled, flabbergasted, Valery was just getting started. "Why did countless scientists waste their lives trying to find a cure for polio? Or for malaria? Or continue to do so for other diseases?" Valery smirked. "Because it's worth the effort. And it's not always about yourself." She stepped behind Sakura and placed her hands on her shoulders. Looking deep into her eyes through the mirror, she added, "Even if we uncover a small stepping stone, Sakura, it will eventually lead those who come behind us to a solution. Making sacrifices to better humankind, Sakura, is a noble pursuit—it's never *wasted time*. Only sitting around wallowing in self-pity and doing nothing is a waste of time."

Sakura sat upright, never having been chided before with such candor, at least not from anyone other than her father. But most teenagers never cared to listen to their parents; the best advice always came from others, or at least many thought so. And Valery's lecture was a refreshing slap in the face.

Sakura nodded. "Okay, okay, I hear you," she said as she picked up the eyeliner pencil and continued to finish her eyebrow. "Even though I have no expectations that we'll discover even a *small* stepping stone, I guess I have nothing to lose." Having finished her eyebrows, she looked at Valery's reflection in the mirror. "I suppose killing time with you for two months is better than killing myself. Right?"

Valery smiled. "Right!" She hugged Sakura from behind and placed her face alongside the older girl's as she gazed excitedly at her in the mirror. "I brought two suitcases with my best science books, along with various specimens, microscopes, and other apparatus. I just need an area where I can set up a lab." She spun around and looked at the spacious bedroom. "I don't know where I could possibly find the space in *this* shack."

Sakura managed to chuckle. "Well, although my room is rather large, we'd best set up shop in the basement." Excitedly, she spun around and looked up at her new friend and co-researcher. "It has an unused section the size of a parking garage, and it's fully furnished."

Valery hugged her tight. "Fantastic!"

The days turned into weeks as the two girls bonded like sisters. Their parents had quickly noticed the change in Sakura's disposition, and the tight union the two girls had forged. While they worked long hours in the laboratory, Valery made several significant breakthroughs with her hybrids. However, the girls also managed to laugh and joke about the silliest of things, and even took long hikes and scenic car rides, as Sakura showed Valery around the countryside and filled her head with tales of the ancient traditions and myths of Japan. Valery was invigorated, and relished how the foreign culture stimulated her mind, as East merged with West.

They traveled to most of the suburbs around Tokyo and beyond, until the seventh week, when Valery noticed a glaring transition. Sakura's appearance was alarming: her once quasi-healthy frame had withered into the skeletal apparition of a ghost, while her stamina had also diminished to that of an elderly woman's.

Valery had all to do to conceal the pain, whether it was the agonizing knots in her stomach that kept her awake at night, or forcing on a warm smile for her dying friend. More painful still was when Sakura courageously mustered a smile in return, which, to Valery, appeared more like a cadaver frowning with rigor mortis. It was clear; Sakura was dying, *fast*.

Valery sat across from Sakura with a few live specimens between them; some of which gave Sakura the shivers, like the rats and large snakes. Also before them were several large beakers and Petri dishes, along with two microscopes. Valery could see Sakura's distorted face through one of the beakers, which was filled with a yellow compound, making her jaundiced face appear even more macabre. Valery knew the cancer was eating Sakura's liver and attacking her red blood cells, and the reality of truly feeling helpless struck her hard. The pain of watching her new best friend wilt away was unbearable. She now questioned her bogus sense of mission that she'd heaped upon Sakura's frail back. *Was she right? Was it all just a waste of time?*

That thought, however, was derailed when Sakura looked at her and pleaded, "I know I shouldn't burden you with this, Val, but all I ask is that you don't tell anyone. I *must* go to *Aokigahara*."

Valery gazed at her dear friend's emaciated face. *How can I deny her last wish? Then again, how can I let her get eaten alive by a terrifying beast—if, in fact, it does exist?*

That very thought switched Valery's gears. If there was such a thing as a multi-genetic *Gorgon*, how could *she* not want to see it herself? Or study it? It would be a Biologist's gold mine.

Valery squinted. "Fine, Sakura. I'll keep quiet, but only if I go along with you. And you must promise not to wander off alone."

Sakura hesitated, then nodded. "I promise."

After a pleasant dinner with their parents, the two girls left the mansion together and arrived at *Aokigahara* two hours later. In the distance, the sun was just beginning to touch the crest of Mount Fuji. Before them stood the dense forest with a labyrinth of narrow dirt paths, morbid trails worn by the weary feet of thousands of desperate souls, all in search of the mystical doorway to another realm.

Valery grasped her large backpack, filled with live specimens and Petri dishes from her laboratory, then clutched Sakura's hand—partially out of loving friendship, partially out of concern for her escaping into the foreboding mist. Nervously, they glanced at each other, then back toward the fading path, as the thick fog eerily distorted their vision and twisted their perceptions like a hallucinogenic drug.

As they weaved deeper and deeper into the forest, pushing their way through a variety of tall conifers, exotic plants, and lichens, Valery gazed down at the liverworts with fascination. "Wow, I've never seen a real liverwort, only in photos."

Sakura followed her line of sight. "Liver wart? Eww! Sounds gross!" She was expecting to see the malignant liver of a dead animal, but then sighed. "Oh, you mean those mossy things?"

Valery giggled, realizing Sakura's initial anxiety, as she bent over and picked off a leaf. "Well, sort of. You see, they look like moss, but they're not. Liverworts have single-celled rhizoids."

Sakura rolled her eyes. "Single-celled rhizoids, of course! I should have known that." She looked at Valery with her dreary gray eyes and tried to smile, but couldn't. "I didn't know you were also a Botanist."

"No, no, liverworts are bryophytes, you silly goose." Valery stuck the leaf in her pocket. "Specialists called Bryologists study them."

Sakura was about to respond with another colorful refrain when they suddenly heard a rustling sound in the bushes. Startled, their heads swiveled in the direction of the noise.

Out of the dense mist a fox emerged. The red little mammal stopped and gazed up at the two intruders, its vibrant little eyes waiting for a response.

Valery sighed with relief as Sakura giggled and looked at Valery. "What a cute little fella, isn't he?"

Suddenly, a large claw swung out of the mist and seized the fox! The girls gasped, as a huge, thorny creature with large, razor-sharp teeth bit into the fox—which shrieked—then tossed its half-eaten carcass to the ground. The twenty-foot tall beast, with its goat-like eyes, gazed eerily at the larger prey before it. The heat of its breath formed swirling clouds of vapor as its nostrils and mouth emitted the vile stench of its rancid lungs, lungs fed with the blood of humans and any unfortunate creature that crossed its path.

Valery and Sakura stood frozen in fear as they gazed up at the towering monstrosity. They could feel the tingling sensation of adrenaline as it rushed through their bodies, while terror strangled their vocal chords. Sakura clutched Valery's hand tighter. She now realized that her previous notion—that of not caring if the *Gorgon* ate her—was a harebrained whim of sheer stupidity.

The menacing beast squinted as it eyed them up, quickly assessing the weakest link. With a snort, it lunged at Sakura and swiped her out of Valery's meager grip. A creepy smile contorted the monster's face as it pivoted, then dashed into the thick mist. In its wake, a swirling cloud of contrails billowed.

Valery screamed, only to hear her horrifying howl drowned out by Sakura's piercing shrieks. Underlying those chilling sounds were the sadistic snickers of the savage beast. Valery dashed after them into the mist, her heart beating with a volatile mixture of fear and vengeance. She could barely see fifteen feet in front of her, but could hear the *Gorgon's* hefty footsteps as they pounded the earth with each thunderous thump. Trees wobbled as roots broke free of the soil and leaves wafted to the ground.

Then, through the mist, Valery saw a horrific sight—the enormous *Gorgon* was hunched over Sakura's dead body, tearing into her flesh. Valery stood frozen, in shock, but intuitively had to scream: "Stop!"

The *Gorgon* flinched and dropped its kill. Gazing at Valery, it licked its lips and stood up. Once again, its distinctive, creepy smile graced its sinister face.

Valery was overwhelmed. The beast was undeniably part humanoid and part bull. It had large horns and seemed to be part dragon, with its scalloped, fleshy mane running down its spine, and smaller ones along each of its arms. Sharp talons eerily protruded out of its massive body in random locations, making for a most hideous sight. Equally daunting was that the beast stood over twenty feet tall, its head hovering among the treetops.

Valery's doubts about Big Foot or the Loch Ness monster were quickly obliterated as she glanced down at her dead friend's gnawed body, then up at the *Gorgon*. Exacerbating her shock and disbelief was when the monster spoke!

"You are fortunate I let you live," the beast said. Tantalizingly, it rubbed its chin with the sharp talon of its index finger. "Why didn't you run away?"

Valery was numb and struggled to regain control of her larynx. She clutched her bulky backpack tightly and uttered, "Because you t-took… I mean, *killed* my fr—" Valery couldn't finish the sentence as she glanced down at Sakura's mangled carcass, then back up at the beast. "Why?" she spat. "You have intelligence, yet you choose to be wicked! What *are* you?"

The *Gorgon* resumed its crouched position, as it mindlessly fiddled with the talons on its deformed neck. "I am the result of *your* race, little missy. And you dare call *me* wicked?" It snorted in disgust as it licked the blood off its clawed fingers. It then snarled and spat, "Look in the mirror, human!" The beast's ugly face turned evermore serious as ugly memories filled its amalgamated mind. "That I should explain what *I* am seems a waste of time, since I *will* kill and eat you. But so be it."

The beast sat upon a felled tree and gazed deeply into Valery's eyes. "It was during your *wicked* World War that Shiro Ishii, a Japanese scientist, experimented with biological warfare. He heartlessly killed many captives, including Chinese babies with lethal injections. Shiro also toyed with genetics and mixed a variety of strains—bulls, warthogs, lions, and vultures—with a human specimen; namely, an American prisoner of war, whom he deemed inferior and suitable for testing. Several months later, the radiation from Hiroshima aided his experiment... and, well, after seventy years or so, *this* is what mankind reaped. *Me!*"

It snarled, then pointed its claw at its repulsive, talon-infested chest. "Humans love to tinker with nature, as if they're smart enough to control it. Yet, the atom unleashed Hell, with radiation spewing into the atmosphere and spoiling your oceans, while your chemicals and preservatives released a profusion of toxins. You even have the audacity to tamper with your own DNA to create something new, as if you could outdo the Master of the Universe. Ha! Fools! All of you!"

Valery's nostrils flared as she retorted, "Yes, we humans make mistakes. But, like this gloomy forest—where you stalk and kill, you see and breathe only darkness, never wise enough to venture into the sunlight. So, you've failed to see and appreciate all the amazing breakthroughs we've made. As we humans say, the road to success is paved with failures...like *you!*"

The *Gorgon* quickly lunged forward and swiped Valery off her feet, clutching her in its clawed hand. Valery screamed; her face now only inches away from the beast's deadly fangs, as its goat-like eyes scanned her from head to toe. The *Gorgon* chuckled, relishing how its prey trembled with fear.

Then the beast squinted as it rubbed its chin. "Again, I must ask. *Why* didn't you run away?" Its vertical slits for pupils widened as they scrutinized her healthy, little body. Its head tilted from side to side as it contemplated which limb it would gnaw first and how tasty it might be. "You're not like those who wander here wishing to end their lives. They're sick, or mentally weak. Human trash!" The beast snarled. "So, why did you stay?"

Valery squirmed, trying to break free of the monster's tight grip, as she retorted, "You could *never* understand. Humans may be flawed, but we have compassion, and would willingly give our own lives to save others, something a cold-hearted killer like *you* could never understand."

The *Gorgon* snarled and couldn't restrain itself any longer. It opened its huge, fanged mouth and attempted to devour her whole. Yet, Valery unzipped her backpack, shoved it in its mouth, and kicked with both feet, each landing squarely in one of its eyes! The *Gorgon* squealed and dropped its catch. Heatedly, it rubbed its throbbing eyeballs while it gagged and swallowed the backpack.

Valery dashed into the mist, just far enough to be out of the *Gorgon's* reach, while the beast spun around, swinging its fists furiously into thin air. "Where are you? You little wretch!"

The savage beast blinked hard to clear its eyes, but all it could see was a blur, as Valery's voice drifted out of the evening mist. "Your days of eating humans are over!"

The *Gorgon* growled as it gazed blindly into the undulating mist. "Over? Never! Once my sight returns, I will hunt you down and *eat you*—slowly, very slowly, so you can experience the agony of death, for *I* am the Master of Death." With a vicious snarl, it spat, "Do you hear me? I *will* kill you, tonight!"

Valery stood firm, as darkness continued to consume the last remnants of twilight. "I think you should know," she retorted. "That backpack you swallowed had a specimen inside—one I recently developed. It's a new breed of eucestoda."

The *Gorgon* continued to swing its fists blindly into the fog, when suddenly, it winced. It grabbed its aching stomach and growled, *"Euces...toda?"*

Valery started to walk backward, calmly, confidently. "It's commonly called a tapeworm. But, I crossbred this one with a boa—it's already six feet long. And, like you, it's extremely carnivorous. It will eat you from the inside out, starting by latching onto your stomach with its multi-pronged mouth hooks. Then it will tear away at you, little by little. I'm sorry to say, the next four hours will be a slow and extremely painful death. But with you being the Master of Death, I can't think of a more fitting way for you to taste what death is *really* like."

The *Gorgon* fell to its knees, terrified and twisting in agony.

With that, Valery turned and ran through the thick mist to retrieve Sakura's ravaged body. Amid the gloomy darkness, only the shrieks of the dying *Gorgon* could be heard as they echoed off the Sea of Trees.

†††

By dawn, Valery had returned to the Hataki mansion, escorted by a procession of police cars, news teams, and elated citizens. As she stepped out of the car, her parents and Riku worriedly ran to greet her amid a flurry of photographers snapping pictures and news commentators reporting the startling headlines:

"VALERY CASELLA, AMERICAN WIZ-KID, KILLS GORGON!"

"MYTHOLOGICAL GORGON, NO MYTH!"

"KID BIOLOGIST FINDS GORGON. WHAT NEXT? BIG FOOT!?"

While one Japanese tabloid Tweeted: "GIRL KILLS GORGON! GODZILLA, BEWARE!"

Peter whisked Valery into Riku's mansion, followed by his wife and Riku, who closed the door behind them.

Riku looked at Valery with a heavy heart, knowing the worst had happened, yet had to ask, as he stuttered, "Was S-Sakura... W-well, I know her t-time was up... B-but did she suffer?"

Valery lied. "No, she went peacefully, Mr. Hataki, in my arms. But I'm sad to say, the Gorgon, well... It picked away at her, after she expired." She could no longer bring herself to recall the horror, and added, "But I retrieved her body for you, so she can be buried respectfully."

Riku sighed as a tear streamed down his face. "I'm very glad that her last days were spent with you, Valery. I hadn't seen her so alive as with you." He paused, then said, "At least her spirit is now at rest with her mother's."

Peter and Angela hugged Valery tight. They had been worried sick when she hadn't come home last night, but were now relieved that they could finally sigh with relief.

Excitedly, Valery looked up at her father. "The authorities said we can take the *Gorgon* home, Dad. Well, not home, but to America for further study, once they inspect it first. It'll be a biological goldmine. I can even do my thesis on it at Johns Hopkins."

Peter smiled, delighted that his daughter proved him wrong and came home a winner after all, while Valery added the icing on the cake. "And get this, I was already contacted by several research labs, each offering to fund further study of this genetic miracle." She paused, then corrected herself. "Or rather—genetic mistake."

†††

Ten days later, the *Gorgon's* valuable cadaver was shipped to Johns Hopkins University, where Valery started her first semester amid a celebratory reception and flashy media headlines.

The cover of the *Johns Hopkins Magazine* featured a photo of Valery standing next to the *Gorgon's* carcass with the title:

"FRESHMAN VALERY CASELLA FINDS THE ELUSIVE GORGON! A BIOLOGIST'S BONANZA!"

Valery went on to enjoy a successful career and notoriety, being awarded the Nobel Prize for, of all things— Evolutionary Biology, as her proud and happily dumbfounded father looked on and applauded his precious daughter.

The Masque

By the looks of it, Victor Laveau literally had it all.

Victor was tall, dark, and not just handsome, but almost unworldly gorgeous. Some townsfolk in New Orleans said it was due to his unique mixture of French, Italian, Native American and African American roots.

Ever since a child, Victor had been adulated profusely: whether by his teachers—who marveled at his almost angelic, sweet face—or by his classmates—the girls swooning as he strut by them, while the boys wished desperately that they had his magnificent, good looks. In fact, many called him Adonis.

However, now at thirty-two years of age, Victor had come to a startling realization; his stunning good looks had been the bane of his life. As he grew older, many people were either too intimidated to approach him, or those who did soon tired of him, as the praise and entitlements he had received for his sterling good looks quickly waned when the blaring reality struck them: namely, Victor's only asset *was* his pretty face. In essence, Victor was a blank slate. He had rested on his lovely laurels his whole, lazy life and never excelled at anything: not school, where he graduated second-to-last in his class; not sports, where he was always the last one picked by his team mates; not the math or chess clubs, neither of which could he figure out; and not even the most basic trades could his inept fingers master.

Dejected and living alone in a small house on Dauphine Street, Victor Laveau was at least fortunate in death—that is, after his parents had died in a car accident twelve years ago he was left with just enough money in the estate to maintain the house and feed himself. Otherwise, Victor's meager salary of a hundred and ten dollars a week—being a part-time groundskeeper at the local Saint Louis Cemetery—would have hurled him into his own grave.

However, as Victor sat on his dead parents' worn-out sofa, looking mindlessly at *Keeping Up with the Kardashians*, his eyes suddenly lit up! An advertisement about the upcoming New Orleans Mardi Gras splashed on the screen, impelling him to sit upright. Having been lost in the numbness of depression for months, Victor had forgotten all about the carnival, or even the Mystic Knights of Adonis parade, which offered him the rare opportunity to flaunt his beautiful face. However, Mardi Gras was the only day each year that truly stimulated his dead and lonely heart, as he could hide his beautiful face behind a masque and not be shunned by the townsfolk, who had chosen long ago to ignore or disparage him. It was Victor's "Get Out of Jail Free" card—at least for a day.

Therefore, the TV ad struck Victor like a taser; Mardi Gras's famous Fat Tuesday was three days away, on February 28, 2017! Victor leapt to his feet and dashed to the mirror. He gazed at the graceful lines of his face: the perfectly chiseled chin, the full luscious lips, the thick head of black hair, the smooth tan skin, and those magnetic blue eyes that had melted many young women's hearts in the past, at least for several minutes, until they realized they were speaking to a pepper-head—colorful outside, hollow inside.

As Victor stared at himself, he knew he had to think of something different this year. Last year's cheap plastic mask had only covered his eyes, and the townsfolk had mocked his chintzy costume, calling it "dull and boring", while Thurston Harrison, the town bully, had even ripped it off his face and crushed it with the heel of his army boot. Not that Thurston was ever in the army, as his only kills were of little animals that he liked to torture or maim first.

Victor stood by the mirror for twenty minutes, frustrated that his mind was blank—creativity never being his strong suit, nor was anything else.

"Damn it, Victor! *Think!*" he growled at his dazzling reflection. "Sometimes I think you're dead already!" Angrily, he pivoted away, but suddenly stopped and turned back toward the mirror. "*Dead.* That's it! A skeleton!" Speaking to himself as if to another person, he continued, "Oh, Victor, Victor, never mind a cheap plastic masque, I'll paint you up so completely, they'll never be able to see an inch of that beautiful skin of yours or be able to pull it off!"

Elated with his novel idea—or so he thought—Victor dashed out to buy face paint. Two days later, when the day arrived, Victor woke up early, ran to the mirror and started to paint his face. He dipped the paintbrush into black paint and splashed it all over his supple skin, closing his eyes one at a time to make sure he covered his eyelids. He waited ten minutes until it dried, then with a fine sable brush, he dipped it in white paint and drew in the bony mandible, cheek bones, and remaining skull on his forehead. He smiled, happy with his creation, and darted out the door.

With a prideful bounce in his step, Victor pranced several blocks to the heart of the French Quarter. As he strolled down Bourbon Street—bustling with people, some laughing and others drinking alcohol—he could smell the spicy Creole food in the air, while his eyes scanned all the fancy and bizarre costumes. He was waiting for a barrage of compliments, but it suddenly hit him; his novel skeleton idea was *not* so novel. In fact, it was painfully common, as hardly anyone acknowledged his presence. Worse still, was the menacing thunderclap that rumbled down from the heavens, while storm clouds gathered and unleashed a deluge of rain.

Victor dashed to gain cover under a fancy wrought-iron balcony and came smack up against a large picture window; his handsome reflection staring back at him, for the rain had washed away his skeletal paint, leaving only a few gray streaks. As others also squeezed under the balcony for shelter, several townsfolk noticed him, as one quipped sarcastically, "Nice costume, pretty boy Laveau!"

While the meanest of the lot, Thurston Harrison, chided, "Go home, Laveau…you Adonis *reject!*"

Victor cowered from the assaults and retreated back to his house. Heatedly, he slammed the door, then marched up to the mirror and barked, "You screw up! You damn, no good, screw up! *You* make me sick!" He grabbed his handsome face with both hands and squeezed it, then twisted it, as if wishing to rip his skin off to reveal the real skeleton underneath.

Adverse to pain, Victor's fingers let go. He stared at his now reddened face and wept. He walked in a daze and slouched into his parent's old worn-out sofa. Dejected, he shook his head as his tear-filled eyes inadvertently landed on his father's bookshelf. He pinched his eyes tight—to eject the tears—then reopened them to see the spine of a book, which read: *The Life of Maria Laveau: The Voodoo Queen.*

Victor was not much of a reader; in fact, not a single book had he opened in the twelve years since his parents died. Even then, they had only been Marvel comic books or a Doc Savage novella.

He reached over and grasped the book. He leaned back and read through several pages, reminding himself of his mysterious ancestor Marie, who had become the most famous practitioner of Voodoo in New Orleans, and perhaps all of America. He had never paid much attention to her, or the rumors of her special powers, as he viewed Voodoo as a joke—or rather, a bad joke. As far as Victor was concerned, it was childish gibberish. He often laughed at all the people going to the *Marie Laveau Museum* in town, and thought they were all lunatics, as he recalled what one old newspaper had said about her: namely, Marie was "the notorious hag who reigns over the ignorant and superstitious as the Queen of the Voodoos."

Being a part-time groundskeeper at Saint Louis Cemetery, Victor was also well aware of how Marie's mausoleum attracted thousands of curious visitors each year to adorn her tomb with flowers, spiritual artifacts, pentagrams, and offer prayers, expecting her to return from the dead, or at least vanquish the evil spirits that haunted their lives.

However, as Victor now sat on the sofa and read through the pages, he could feel his brain's amazing transformation: the rust of self-pity was slowly dissolving, as a surge of confidence now cleansed and awakened his senses. The stories of Marie's startling abilities he now found intriguing. He never knew that her craft, which many from all stations in life sought, combined African Voodoo with Roman Catholicism. Three hours later, he slid the book back into its slot on the shelf, and resolved himself to studying hard over the next year. His goal: to make the most unique masque New Orleans had ever seen!

Over the ensuing months Victor read books on woodcarving, metal sculpture, glassworks, and consumed the illustrated books of famous fine artists: yet not those who painted realism, impressionism, or abstraction, but those who explored the cosmic horizons of the imagination, such as Salvador Dali, M.C. Escher, Frank Frazetta, H.R. Giger, and others.

For months he sat at the dinette table with paper and pencil and drew hundreds of sketches of strange masques. Yet none, he felt, were bizarre enough. He gazed up at the calendar: he had four months until Mardi Gras. Yet it suddenly struck him: he was thirty-two and would be thirty-three on the day of the next Mardi Gras—the same age that Jesus died. Moreover, the festival happened to fall of February 13! With his new awareness and reverence for spiritualism and superstitions, he now had reservations; would he, at 33, die on the 13th? Or be crucified, figuratively speaking, somehow?

Victor grasped a cup of hot cocoa and sat pondering these ominous thoughts as he sipped and stared into space for several minutes. Then he slammed the empty cup down and picked up a pencil, sketching one masque after another: altering the shape of the lips here, the eyes there, or replacing a commonplace feature with something more unnatural, yet always keeping a fine balance of maintaining a somewhat humanoid face, one that was ugly, yet artistic. Then with a final stroke of his pencil, Victor smiled. He was finished. He created the winner!

He dashed down the street and purchased a variety of materials and tools at Mel's Hardware Store, and then set to work. Diligently, Victor grasped a large piece of pinewood and a chisel, and carved the skeletal framework, then used clay to mold the droopy cheeks and eyelids. He fired up the small rented furnace and formed the two penetrating, glass eyeballs with cat-like pupils. Carefully, he shaped several nuggets of bronze into talons, which he placed on the masque's ugly cheeks and head. Next, he pulled out his scissors and cut up purple silk fabric to form an odd bat-like drape that he hung between the nose and mouth. For the final touches, he whittled oak to form its sharp little teeth, and even used white Styrofoam to craft an egg, which he placed on its head. The egg, Victor believed, symbolized his long-awaited rebirth, a rebirth that would soon occur through the mystical power of his masterpiece—his *ugly* masterpiece. For Adonis would at last find fame and fortune via deformity.

With the last-minute touch ups of painting the needle-like teeth white and the droopy cheeks magenta, Victor stood back and admired his ugly, artistic masterpiece. A huge grin enlivened his handsome face. Victor hadn't felt so alive and confident in all of his useless life, and he eagerly set about slipping into a pair of black pants, a black shirt, and black shoes. There was no need, he knew, to bring attention anywhere else; his unique and ugly masque would unquestionably command the scene, as it would dominate everyone's attention and garner the admiration and respect he so desperately craved and deserved.

Adrenaline ran through Victor like nitromethane through a dragster, with all pistons firing at high octane. Excitedly, he slipped the ugly masque over his handsome face, bolted out the door, and raced down the streets. As he arrived at Bourbon Street, he slowed down to a proud and steady beat, as onlookers gasped and gaped in awe. Youngsters recoiled in horror and clutched their mothers' skirts or fathers' arms, while adults of all ages marveled at the bizarre apparition.

Underneath that ugly masque, however, Victor's gorgeous face beamed with delight, as crowds flocked around him, offering high praise or bulleting him with questions, as one man asked, "Oh my God! Where did you buy that masque? It's fantastic!"

"Thank you, good sir," Victor replied. "But, *this* masque is unique. It can't be purchased anywhere."

Meanwhile, a mother, whose scared daughter clung to her hip, inquired, "Dear Lord! Did *you* make that?"

"Yes, ma'am. I most certainly did. It's one of a kind."

"It's grossly… magnificent! Yes, hideous, yet oddly appealing somehow."

Victor cordially thanked her and all his admirers as he continued to strut through the crowd like a movie star: adulated by fans, yet oddly enough, ugly as sin. He couldn't get over it; the reactions were as bizarre as his masque. Nevertheless, Victor savored the moment as if Lord Voldemort—ugly, but wildly popular.

But as Victor turned the corner, his heart began to race; the moment he had waited for arrived, as Thurston Harrison pushed his way through the crowd and approached him. Victor gazed through the huge glass orbs of the masque, waiting anxiously for his obnoxious neighbor's response: did he recognize him or not?

Thurston shook his head in amazement. "Damn! That's gotta be the coolest mask I ever laid eyes on!" He reached into his backpack filled with beers and ice, pulled out a Corona and extended it to the eerie specter before him. "You look like Death itself. I'd be honored if you'd have a drink on me."

Victor hesitated; he seriously wanted to pour the drink *on* him, but then he thought of Marie Laveau and her Voodoo/Christian powers. What he had learned was that they weren't sinister spells, as many sought Marie out to heal the sick, enhance their lives with positive vibes, or exorcize evil spirits. Victor shrugged his shoulders. "Sure, why not, how could I refuse anyone who honors *me*?"

Victor grasped the bottle and slipped it through the large gap between the masque's nose and its mouth: the mouth being located a foot below the nose by a thin skeletal bone and sat at the middle of Victor's chest. Locating his real mouth, Victor took a healthy swig.

As the minutes rolled into hours, more and more people gathered around Victor in awe and walked along side him down Bourbon Street. As they paraded among the city's unique French and Spanish Creole architecture, the sounds and smells of its world-renowned music and Creole cuisine filled the air. Meanwhile, out-of-towners and his once nasty neighbors all bought the sensational masquerader one drink after another: a Budweiser here, a shot of Jack Daniels there, a Corona, a Heineken, and so it went.

Victor Laveau was in a state of euphoria. *This* Mardi Gras was the pinnacle of his life. People from all walks of life praised him and asked all sorts of questions:

"How did you make the masque?"

"Where did you get the idea?"

"Could you make me one?"

Surrounded by an adoring mob, Victor gave out autographs, posed to take pictures with fans, and even offered his phone number to a few people who had an interest in having masques designed for next year's gala. One entrepreneur, Nick Marcello, pushed his way through the crowd and handed Victor his business card. He leaned toward his ear and whispered, "I'd love to partner up with you, or at least license the design for my fledgling costume company. We can make millions!"

Victor was on cloud nine, as he replied, "I'm rather busy right now—" he glanced at the card, "*Nick*. But I'll call you." He stuffed the card in his pocket and winked.

As admirers pushed and shoved Victor deeper into the frenzied mob, Marcello tipped his hat and weaved back toward the parade.

Meanwhile, many hours passed as Victor drank one complimentary drink after another. His bloodshot eyes rolled to the sluggish sea of suds in his head as 4 AM rolled around. Victor bid his new friends good night, and staggered homeward. Ossified and disoriented, Laveau lost his bearings and proceeded to wobble through a series of dark alleys, while whistling or singing silly songs along the way. Regardless of the slurred speech and butchered lyrics, Victor was elated—he did it! He was a success.

†††

Victor woke up, disoriented, as he lay on his back in a strange alley. He gazed lazily upward at the dawn sky, only to see a towering figure standing above him. The mysterious shape blocked the sunlight and cast a shadow over his bewildered face.

Victor squinted, waiting for his eyes to adjust and focus on the dark blue silhouette above him.

The policeman finally spoke: "Get up! You're under arrest!"

Victor blinked hard and shook his head, causing the sea of suds to crash into the side of his skull, creating a pool of pain. Slowly, he sat upright, holding his throbbing head, as he uttered, "I'm s-sorry for loitering, officer. B-but, must you arrest me? It's M-mardi Gras, for Christ's s-sake."

The policeman pulled out his pistol. "I said, *get the hell up!*"

Another officer approached. "Is this the dirty bastard you radioed me about, Jim?"

Victor's head recoiled. "Dirty b-bastard? *Me?*"

"Yeah, *you!* You prick. Don't play dumb," Jim spat, losing his patience.

"I d-don't under-sstand," Victor said with his lazy, liquored tongue. "What's t-this all a-about?"

Jim's partner shook his head. "Come off it, asshole. I was told you were caught red-handed." He glanced at the masque lying next to the drunkard on the cobblestone alley. "And there's your ugly masque that my partner told me about."

Jim added, "And we have a witness, too. You'll be toast, soon enough, Laveau. So, get your ass up, so I can cuff you."

With that, Jim kicked Victor's shoe, while his partner read Victor his Miranda rights.

Victor looked over, grasped his masque out of the gutter, and wobbled up to his feet. He gazed at officer Jim. "How'd you know m-my n-name?"

"Never mind, Victor. We know everything."

"If that's s-so, then do you m-mind telling me *w-what* you're arresting me for?"

Jim's lips twisted as he glanced at his partner. "Don't you hate it, Bob, when these dirt bags play dumb?" He looked back at Victor. "Let me refresh your *Ale*-ing memory, Mr. Lowenbrau. You murdered Mel Thornton, proprietor of Mel's Hardware Store."

"*What!?*" Victor shrieked, as adrenaline rushed to his head. "That's im-ppossible! You have t-the w-wrong guy. I s-swear."

Jim shook his head as he once again looked at Bob. "When the hell will these idiots come up with new lines?" Cringing like a whimpering child, Jim mimicked: "You have the w-wrong guy. I s-swear. I'm innocent, officer, really I am, I swear!" He looked back at Victor. "Guys like *you* make me sick, Laveau! I knew Mel, he was a seventy-four-year-old gentleman and respectable businessman in our neighborhood. Then a punk like *you* comes along and caps him. For what? To steal a hundred and forty dollars from his register. Is that what a man's life is worth to you?"

Victor was still zonked by the alcohol, but now felt nauseous. He listed toward officer Jim, then vomited—the vile chunky liquid jettisoning out of his body and splattering Jim's trousers and shoes.

"Ah, shit!" Jim bellowed. He looked at Bob. "Cuff Linda Blair, while I clean up."

Bob whipped his handcuffs around Victor's wrists and walked him to the squad car. Victor wiped his soiled mouth on his shoulder, and again pleaded, "I'm t-telling you, officer. I d-didn't do it. I w-wasn't even t-there. I s-swear!"

"Sure you weren't. By the smell of your breath, Victor, I'd say you could have been *anywhere* and not remember. But the party's over. You killed Mel Thornton. *And*, an eyewitness saw you, who happens to know you. So this is a pretty open and shut case." He placed his hand on Victor's head and carefully lowered him into the backseat. "Now I advise you to shut up and enjoy the ride."

With that, officers Bob and Jim drove Victor down to the precinct.

†††

Three weeks later, Victor was sitting in a courtroom before the Honorable Judge Loren Baker. At Victor's side was his appointed court attorney, Jacque Pardue, who sat shuffling papers in his disheveled, hand-me-down suit.

Meanwhile, District Attorney Bill Burgess had grilled the only two character witnesses Pardue produced. With his flair for melodrama, Burgess had chided them for having defended a murderer and drilled into the jurors' heads that officer Jim Kelly's report was substantiated by an eyewitness.

Jacque Pardue had only half-listened, as his daughter's first birthday party weighed heavier on his mind than this oddball, whom many local citizens had eagerly testified against, citing his strange reclusive lifestyle and grave-digging fascination as evidence of a warped mind. The rookie attorney looked at Victor and whispered, "Listen, Victor, Louisiana carries the death penalty. So your life rests in *your* hands. Take the stand. Get up there and defend yourself!"

Unwittingly, Victor rose from his chair and approached the bench. He swore on the Bible and confidently took the stand, eager to settle this with the truth, once and for all.

Burgess, who was as rotund as Orson Welles and feisty as DA Jim Garrison, wasted no time and went on the attack. "So, Mr. Laveau, as I clearly stated for the court, the events that occurred at Mardi Gras on February thirteenth were that, you fashioned a ghastly masque, which garnered great attention." He glanced at the jury. "I'd like to expand on this first part of the exposition, because it's quite important."

Fixing his piercing brown eyes back on Victor, he continued, "After all, with your infamous Voodoo ancestor being Marie Laveau, and your *bad luck* occurring on the *thirteenth*, I'd say bad luck is a family trait. Isn't that so, Mr. Laveau?"

Victor gazed at Burgess, who appeared to resemble a bulldog and, evidently, bit like one, too. "No. Allow me to correct you," Victor said with poise. "Actually, sir, I was told that the *alleged* murder occurred at six-thirteen in the morning, on February *fourteenth*."

Burgess snarled; he rarely made such mistakes, but opted to press on. "Whatever. The point *is*: you walked into Mel Thornton's hardware store that morning, wearing your custom-made Voodoo mask, asked him for all his money, then went to open his register. In response, Mr. Thornton *rightfully* pulled out his licensed revolver, which he kept under his counter for such occasions. *However*, you wrestled it out of his hands and shot him!"

Turning toward the jury, he elaborated, "Yes, Victor Laveau shot and killed Mel Thornton. And for what? A measly one hundred and forty dollars. Then he ran out the door. Yet the drunken murderer collapsed in an alley, only to be caught by officer Jim Kelly, who, moments before, had been alerted to the crime by Clara Parker's scream, who had witnessed the murder."

"That's *not* what happened!" Victor blurted, losing his patience. "I wasn't even in Mel's store!"

"Mr. Laveau. Clara Parker—your neighbor for twenty years—just so happened to walk in the store that morning. She *saw you!* In fact, you bumped into her on your mad dash to flee the scene of your cold-blooded crime." Burgess's lips curled. "So, how do you explain *that*?"

"I can't, sir. Because I don't remember being there."

"Ah!" Burgess exclaimed, as his eyes widened. "How convenient. You don't remember. Do you have an alibi? A witness, perhaps, who saw you elsewhere that morning?"

"Not that I'm aware of, sir. But I don't remember because I drank an awful lot that night. Evidently, I blacked out."

Burgess laughed. "Yes, *evidently*," he said while glancing at the jury. "Like I said, how convenient. But the fact of the matter is, Clara Parker *did* see you, and, at that moment, you weren't lying in the alley blacked out, Mr. Laveau, because you were in Mel Thornton's store. It's also a known fact that you work as a part-time groundskeeper and gravedigger at Saint Louis Cemetery, making only a hundred and ten dollars a week. So by your standards, the hundred and forty dollars you made on that *one* morning was a *killing*—on all accounts! *Right*, Mr. Laveau?"

"*Wrong!* Mr. Burgess."

"Allow me to piece this all together for you, Mr. Laveau. You had the *motive*: the need for money. We have the *weapon*, with your fingerprints on it. And we have an *eyewitness*, who not only saw you, but knows you, Mr. Laveau. There isn't a single piece missing in this puzzle. Not one!"

Victor cracked his neck and huffed. "*Wrong*, again. There are *two* pieces missing! First: I don't need money; I inherited my parents' estate. So there's *no* motive. Second: as I told you, I blacked out because it was Mardi Gras. Many people got plastered that night. But I'm not a drinker, sir. So, I admit, it knocked me for a loop." Victor leaned forward. "How could someone in *that* condition do anything?"

Burgess shook his hefty head. "Mr. Laveau, I can believe you're not a drinker if you don't know the full effects of a blackout. It doesn't necessarily mean a person is out cold. A person *can* fully function: they can talk, walk, dance, drive a car, almost anything. However, they'll have no recollection of those activities when they regain consciousness. Hence, the term blackout!" Burgess cracked a subtle smile; knowing he now had Victor right where he wanted him, as he said, "Therefore, let me rephrase it for you. Is it *possible* that you did it, and don't remember?"

Victor didn't bat an eye. "No!"

Burgess squinted; it wasn't the answer he expected. "Why is that?"

"Because I'm *not* a killer, sir. I wouldn't hurt a fly, never did. And there are plenty of them buzzing around the cemetery."

Burgess rolled his eyes and gritted his teeth. He needed to lure him into answering correctly, and he should have had it by now. "But, since you couldn't remember, Mr. Laveau, is it *possible*?"

Victor bit his lips as he thought it over. "Well, anything's possible, I suppose. But—"

"*Thank you!* That's all, Mr. Laveau!" Burgess exclaimed as he buoyantly pivoted around with the grace of a three-legged elephant. Facing the jurors, he straightened out his Luca Falcone 3XL suit and said, "You heard it from his own lips—*anything is possible*. You saw and heard all the evidence: the motive, his need for money; the weapon, the pistol in Exhibit A; the eyewitness, who, without a shadow of a doubt, saw him; and the testimony of police officer Jim

Kelly, who arrived on the scene and found Victor Laveau lying in the alley with his hand-made Death Masque: the one-of-a-kind face-mask that Laveau wore when he held up Mel Thornton's hardware store and shot him *dead* for a hundred and forty dollars!"

Victor went numb, as if his whole body were injected with Novocain. He tried to speak, but couldn't, as Burgess looked at the jurors and hammered the last nail in Laveau's coffin. "Furthermore, my fellow citizens, it's imperative that you recall the ten character witnesses at the outset of this trial. As they clearly stated, they have known Victor Laveau anywhere from ten to thirty years, and all agreed: Victor Laveau is, and always has been, an odd ball: a loner, an unstable recluse, often sullen and prone to depression, a deadbeat obsessed with the occult. This child relative of notorious Voodoo worshiper and black-arts queen, Marie Laveau—who even crafted the most bizarre and hideous masque that New Orleans, nay, *possibly the world* has ever seen—obviously has pure evil in his DNA."

Burgess pulled out a hankie and wiped his fat, sweaty forehead, then walked up to the jury box and placed his meaty paws on the railing. Leaning forward, he said, "We even found Voodoo dolls in his home, which you saw in Exhibit B, and presented several neighbors who accused him of casting evil spells on them. Why? Because they *allegedly* spoke ill of him... *him*, Victor Laveau: the weirdo, the wacko, the *warlock!* Who *wouldn't* speak ill of *him!*? This menace to society, this crazy cretin, this vicious murderer!"

He pointed heatedly at the defendant. "Victor Laveau must *never* be allowed to walk the streets of our good city, or stalk its innocent citizens, ever again!" Burgess's bulldog eyes scanned each juror's face. "As such, it's imperative that you find Victor Laveau guilty of murder on all accounts and request the death sentence!" He paused for added effect, then concluded, "Remember, my friends, the only way to rid us of evil…is to *terminate* evil!"

Victor sat mute and paralyzed with shock. He couldn't believe the vile and scary picture painted of him. He was painted to look like some hideous alien being by this H.R. Giger of DAs. It was terrifying, as he barely managed to glance at his attorney, who sheepishly buried his head into his case folder and feigned being busy.

As the jurors were instructed to leave their seats and deliberate, Victor sat dazed and holding his throbbing head. To his further dismay, it was only fifteen minutes, when the jurors returned. In horror, Victor listened to the final verdict as a lump welled in his throat.

"We find the defendant guilty of first-degree murder," said the head juror.

Victor felt nauseous, as the Honorable Loren Baker declared, "Victor Laveau, judged by your peers, the State of Louisiana has found you guilty of first-degree murder. And having witnessed first-hand your refusal to admit your guilt amid the overwhelming evidence presented, I duly sentence you to death by lethal injection."

Victor keeled over and vomited.

Laveau was carted to the Louisiana State Penitentiary in West Feliciana Parish. Surrounded by the Mississippi River on three sides, some called it the *Alcatraz of the South*. However, most simply called it *Angola*, being that it was built over the Angola Plantation that used to import its slaves from Angola, Africa.

Dejectedly, Victor sat in his cell, on tier F on Death Row. He couldn't believe the chain of events that brought him to this dank and dingy pit, nor could he believe that he killed Mel Thornton, even *if* he were blacked-out. He sat on his metal bunk staring at the cement floor as his hands gripped his ailing head. With a grunt, he tugged on his hair. *How could I have done it?* his mind squealed. *I knew Mel. I bought all my crafting tools from him.* Bought *them, not* stole *them.* He shook his head. *I don't need a lot of money, never did. This doesn't make sense.*

He released the tight grip on his hair, then squinted. *And what* exactly *did Clara Parker see that morning?* He sat upright. *She said she saw me. Yet, I was wearing the masque. So she didn't really see* me. *So whom* did *she see?* He scratched his chin. *As Mr. Burgess would say, isn't it* possible *that someone took my masque while I was blacked out in the alley, killed Mel, then returned it to me… to frame me?* Victor gritted his teeth. *Christ, I was the perfect stooge, a scapegoat!* Suddenly, a disturbing thought flashed in his head: *Could it have been Thurston Harrison?*

Three days later, Victor clutched a piece of chalk and crossed out another box on the calendar, each daily box getting closer to the one with the big red X, marked for D-day, or April 23. It was April 5 and the prospect of death weighed heavily on his mind.

However, three days ago, Victor had called Nick Marcello, owner of the fledgling costume company. They had become friends since Mardi Gras and Victor asked him for an odd request: specifically, a piece of hair or a possession of each of the four people who were at the crime scene, those being, Clara Parker, officers Jim Kelly and Bob Hansen, and the corpse: Mel Thornton.

Nick had at first thought Victor was jesting or had gone insane, but soon changed his mind once Victor explained his transformation, which had occurred over the past year while studying his great ancestor Marie. It had not only opened Victor's eyes but also his senses and abilities to otherworldly dimensions, aspects of himself that he never realized he had. Nick readily conceded, especially since Victor's trial and conviction had made headline news across the nation, while interest in Victor's "Death Masque"—as it had been dubbed—had skyrocketed. That Nick would become his partner—or at least acquire licensing rights to the masque if he helped Victor prove his innocence—significantly boosted his motivation. Added to Victor's request was that Nick should bring him the four Voodoo dolls he had made during the trial and kept at his house.

Nick walked toward Victor's cell with the box—which had been x-rayed and physically inspected by security—and handed it to him.

Victor grasped the parcel eagerly. "Thank you, Nick. This box is a life saver, literally."

Nick shook his head. "I don't know how you can be so sure, Victor. Me personally, I don't believe in this whole Voodoo nonsense. I just like the money I make from selling ugly masks and crazy costumes. But your partnership offer, or licensing deal, lured me into this crazy scheme." Nick sat on the bunk beside him. "As you requested, I managed to get samples from each: I followed the two officers to Starbucks and swiped their empty coffee cups; I intentionally bumped into Clara on the street and asked her for two fives for a ten; and I happen to know the owner of the funeral home where Mel was waked, so getting a sample was a piece of cake—or rather, a piece of hair."

Victor chuckled. "That's fantastic, Nick. You did good."

Nick peered down at the four Voodoo dolls. "S-sooo what exactly do you plan to do with... *them*?"

Victor smiled. "Each one, once pinned with the specific trinket that you collected, will become a spiritual representation of the corresponding person. As I mentioned, over the past year, I've studied and practiced Voodoo, and just recently I've unleashed the powers within me to see visions and connect with people through these dolls."

Nick laughed. "Yeah, I get it. Just like in the old movies, like *Comin' Round the Mountain*, when Lou Costello and Margaret Hamilton have a hilarious fight by sticking pins into Voodoo dolls of each other. You're a real laugh and a half, Victor."

"Okay, if you say so. But it's not so funny. At first, I didn't believe it myself, but I suppose I just have the right DNA for it."

Nick's grin withered. "So, you're serious?"

"I am. After all, *I am* a Laveau." Strumming his air-guitar, he added, "Like Jimi Hendrix said, *I'm a Voodoo Child. Lord knows I'm a Voodoo Child!*"

Nick managed to chuckle as he shook his head. "Well, for your sake, I hope so." He patted his thighs, anxious to leave, being uncomfortable in a prison cell. "Well, if you need anything else, give me a call. You know I want you exonerated as much as you do. Right, *potential* partner?"

Victor smiled. "Sure I do. And not *potential*, just *impending* partner."

Nick twisted his lips and shrugged, not convinced. He got up, embraced Victor, then called for the guard, who escorted him out of the prison.

No sooner did Nick leave, than Victor eagerly pinned officer Jim's paper coffee cup to one doll, officer Bob's cup to another, Clara's five-dollar bills to another, and Mel's hair to the last doll's head.

He picked up Mel's effigy and stared deep into its two round beads for eyes. He touched its head, rubbing Mel's hair as he closed his eyes. Willing himself into a deep trance, Victor pressed the Voodoo doll against his forehead, melding his consciousness with the transcendental mysteries of Mel's departed spirit. For twenty minutes he sat gently rocking to and fro with the doll pressed tightly to his head, when suddenly a dim flicker of light appeared in the darkness of his mind. A faint dreamy vision slowly materialized. As Victor intensified his concentration, his whole body began to quake as images flashed across the theater of his mind, when, suddenly, he was jolted awake by a shocking image!

He pushed the Voodoo doll away and gazed at the crude effigy of Mel. He shook his head and wiped the sweat off his brow as his heart raced. He couldn't believe any of it; the fact that he had such a powerful vision and, more astoundingly, *what* he saw.

Victor rubbed his pulsing temple as his mind reeled: *Did I really connect with Mel's mind through his spirit? Or was the vision I just saw a fabrication of what I wanted to see?* He scratched his head. *No! That's not what I wanted to see, I had no expectations. And dear God, that image! That damn image!*

He turned his gaze toward the Voodoo doll of officer Jim Kelly. "You son of a bitch!"

Over the next three days Victor embraced each of the three remaining Voodoo dolls, focusing all his energies on one effigy per day. With his eyes closed, Victor had communed telepathically with the two police officers and eyewitness, whereby he received vivid images about their recollections of that fateful morning. Victor was mortified at what he saw, and once he organized all four separate visions in his mind, the entire chain of events fell into place and played like a live video, which Victor now saw vividly:

At 6:05 AM that morning, officer Jim Kelly walked into Mel's Hardware Store. "Good morning, *Mel*." He said with a sardonic bite. "You're three months behind."

Mel's eyes bulged; he didn't expect Jim so early. He wanted to dash out the back door, but it was too late. "Listen, Jimmy, you gotta give me more time. I've been hit hard with my wife's oncology bills, and I—"

"I don't care to hear your bellyaches, Mel. We all have problems, and if I let every one of you whiny weasels off the hook, where would that put *me*?"

Mel nervously edged his way toward the counter and discreetly slid his shaking hand underneath. As he spoke, he opened the drawer. "But you make a good salary, Jim, and you make a pretty penny off of every business owner in town." A bead of sweat dripped down the side of his face. "Moreover, you're a cop for Christ's sake, you'll have a great pension once you retire in a few years."

Mel placed his gnarled hand on the pistol; he was well aware that Jim had brutally battered Hamid—the Dunkin Donut's owner next door—for being two months late, and Mel had enough. Especially that the love of his life was slipping into the next world, Mel had little left to live for and wasn't about to swallow anymore crow from a rat bastard like Jim Kelly.

Purging his fear with raw vengeance, Mel spat, "I have *no* pension, and pretty soon *no* wife. So, *you* can eat shit, Jimbo!"

Mel pulled out the pistol, but Jim had already observed the old man's nervous tell signs and lunged at him. Before Mel knew it, he was on the floor wrestling with the agile cop. Jim manhandled the pistol out of Mel's hand and rammed it straight between his eyes. "You dirty ol' piece of shit! You have the balls to try and kill *me*!? Well, eat *this*!"

With a pull of the trigger, the gun recoiled with a pop as a chunk of lead bore through Mel's forehead into his brain. The ghastly sight even ruffled Jim as his senses rushed back into his hothead. He looked around to see if anyone was present, but he was the first one to stroll in that morning. He darted to the front door, locked it, and flipped the "Open" sign around to "Closed", then pulled out his private cell phone. As he punched the speed dial for his mistress, he shut off the store lights.

"Hello? Clara?"

"Uh, yeah, Jim," she said with a yawn. "What has you calling me at this early hour? Is Janet on to us?"

"No, no, just listen. Hurry over to Mel's Hardware Store A-SAP!"

"What's wrong!? You sound terrified."

"I can't explain, but... oh, shit, I really messed up this time, sweetie. Just get here, *fast!*"

Clara was well accustomed to her lover's hot temper and penchant for fighting, and, by the sound of his frazzled voice, suspected he had really done it this time. "I'll be right there, sweetheart. Don't worry, we'll clean this mess up, somehow."

Fifteen minutes later, Clara stepped into the store and into a world of bad, as her eyes bulged at the bloody corpse on the floor. "Oh, shit!"

Jim was still wiping the blood off his face with a paper towel. "Tell me about it!" He glanced down at the body. "This old piece of shit tried to shoot me."

Clara sighed. "Well, then it was self defense. You have nothing to worry about."

Jim shook his head. "Well, the thing is...I c-can't say a word about this." He stammered. "You see, I was sort of squeezing him for dough, and—"

Clara's pretty face wilted. "You stupid imbecile! Why? Why would you need to do such a thing?"

Jim snarled. "Don't give me your Mother Teresa bullshit, Clara! You have expensive tastes: for jewelry, clothes, cuisine, and all those designer bags I pissed away my money on. And don't forget how my wife and three kids suck me dry. I need the extra cash just to keep up with all of you. You're all killing me!"

"Killing *you*!" Clara retorted with piercing eyes. "You mean *you* killing innocent people!"

Jim pointed adamantly at the body. "We don't have time for this nonsense, we have to do something with this heap of shit, *and quick.*"

Clara gazed at the wrinkled old carcass lying in a pool of blood and closed her eyes. Irritably, she shook her head and huffed, then, as if the Mega Millions winner, her eyes opened as she looked up at Jim. "I don't believe it, but today's your lucky day."

Jim snarled. "*Lucky*, my ass. Cut the crap! Do you have any ideas or not?"

"Yes, I wasn't teasing you. In fact, I have an excellent idea." Her face and body became animated. "On my way here I saw my *loser* neighbor, drunk as a skunk, in an alley, out cold."

"Yeah? So what?"

"So, run there, you big lummox, get his finger prints on the pistol, then get back here ASAP and toss it on the floor next to Mel. The drunken fool is even wearing a masque, so it will look like a hold up." As Jim's face began to beam, she added, "I'll keep a look out and make sure no one comes in."

Jim leaned over and kissed her. "You're the best!" Eagerly, he wiped the gun clean with another paper towel as Clara briefly explained the weird tales about her weird neighbor, who was now lying in an alley, two blocks away.

Jim darted out the door and, ten minutes later, returned. He placed the gun on the floor and looked at Clara. "Ok, *witness*, go home. I'll call you later. Love ya!"

As they exited the store, they kissed and parted ways, as he made his way back to the alley to arrest Victor. He radioed his partner, and minutes later, officer Bob arrived on the scene; an innocent pawn to Jim and Clara's sinister scheme.

Sitting on death row while these vivid images rattled his head, Victor sprang up and summoned the guard, who escorted him to the phone. He called Nick Marcello and, once again, asked him to do some legwork: namely, call the two eyewitnesses he'd seen in his vision who saw Clara Parker leave her apartment at 6:15 that morning. Which happened to be two minutes *after* Mel was killed.

Nick drove the two witnesses to the police station, where they were duly questioned. Clara was brought in, and it didn't take long for her to break down. Clara revealed the entire plot, partly due to a burning incentive: Jim had broken off the affair, fearing their relationship, if discovered, might implicate them, not to mention the fear if his wife Janet found out about the affair.

On April 21, Victor Laveau was sitting in his cell, gazing nervously at his calendar. It was just two days before D-day. The guard appeared, pulled out his keys and opened the cell door. Nick walked in.

"Well, I have bad news, Vic."

Victor's worried face turned pasty white.

"You're a free man!" Nick bellowed. "You got the governor's pardon!"

Victor sprang up and shouted, "Yes! Yes! Yes!" He

gazed back at the calendar and tore it off the wall. He ripped it into shreds and threw the pieces up, like confetti. With a luminous grin, he turned and hugged Nick. "Thanks for all your help, buddy!"

Nick smiled. "No problem, *partner!*"

†††

The sensational story hit the news and Victor Laveau became a national celebrity. He opened his own *Psychic Voodoo Shop* in the French Quarter, where he enhanced the lives of thousands by his prescient advice, while also solving criminal cases for the New Orleans Police Department.

People from all over the world flocked to see him and take photographs with the stunningly handsome psychic, who had also acquired a wide network of friends.

Victor and Nick Marcello became partners in their new joint costume venture and earned seven figures in the first year alone, selling Victor's exclusive designs, with the best seller being a forgone conclusion: namely, Victor's wildly famous—and uniquely hideous—Death Masque.

Celebrating their first anniversary of success, Victor sat at a lavish table, full of the finest gourmet foods, in his new mansion along with Nick and a cadre of friends. With a grin and a warm heart, Victor stood up and embraced Nick. As he did, his eye caught a glimpse of his famous Death Masque on the wall, causing him to reflect on the strange chain of events; for, quite ironically, unlike *King Kong,* where beauty killed the beast, here a beastly masque had brought beauty and joy into his life. With a toast and good cheer, Victor and friends laughed and enjoyed a glorious evening, being just one of many.

Thank You

With this being my second venture into writing a collection of speculative fantasy and sci-fi works, I am indebted to all those writers and film script authors who have influenced me over many years. From Rod Serling and his spectacular group of writers of the *Twilight Zone*, to Gene Roddenberry, Ray Bradbury, George Lucas, and George R.R. Martin, and the many others, I thank you!

To my steadfast family and friends, and of course my dear readers, who have supported my creative endeavors, along with my editors, marketers, and to all the contest judges who have voted several of my books as award winners, including the Best Book Cover Award for *Short Stories III: Strange, Weird and Sci-Fi*, I am most grateful.

Thank you!

— Rich DiSilvio

My Nazi Nemesis

GOLD AWARD WINNER

★★★★★ **"DiSilvio's plot is cunning and ingenious!"**
-- Jack Magnus for Readers' Favorite

A deadly love triangle launches a father and daughter team to hunt down a nefarious Nazi. Yet twists and turns abound, leading to a shocking climax.

Hardcover: 9780981762586
Paperback: 9780981762579
eBook: 9780981762593

A Blazing Gilded Age

INTERNATIONAL AWARD WINNER AND BEST COVER DESIGN

A riveting rags-to-riches saga about a poor family's struggle to survive amid a nation burning with ambition yet bleeding with injustice. Features, Teddy Roosevelt, JP Morgan, Mark Twain, Tesla and more.

Lauded by HISTORY/A+E and noted biographer Roger DiSilvestro.

Hardcover: 9780981762562
Paperback: 9780981762555
eBook: 9780997680720

Tales of Titans Series

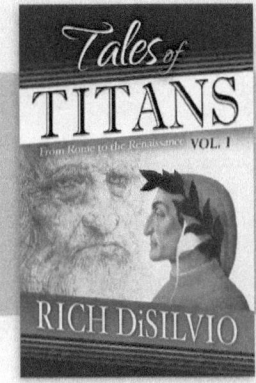
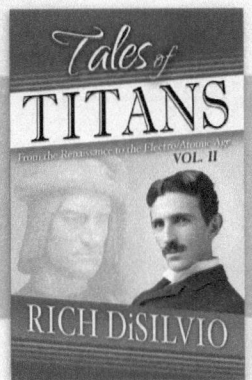

Tales of Titans brings great historical figures to life with concise yet compelling essays, coupled with engaging narratives that enlighten readers to their miraculous deeds, and misdeeds, that have significantly shaped Western civilization.

This handsomely illustrated series offers readers brief biographical overviews and cogent analysis, while the quasi-fictional scenarios transport readers into a fascinating past, whereby putting flesh on the bones of several titans and offering glimpses into their hearts, minds, and actions.

Tales of Titans, Vol. I : From Rome to the Renaissance
Augustus & Livia, Vespasian & Titus, Hadrian, Constantine, Dante, Brunelleschi, Columbus, Vespucci, King Ferdinand, Pope Alexander VI & Cesare Borgia, and Leonardo da Vinci.

Tales of Titans, Vol. II: Renaissance to the Electro/Atomic Age
The Medicis, Gutenberg, Lorenzo de Medici, Savonarola, Leonardo & Machiavelli, Martin Luther, Queen Elizabeth I, Shakespeare, Galileo, Darwin, Marx, Stalin, Freud, Marconi, Edison, Tesla, Westinghouse, Einstein, Fermi and von Braun.

Tales of Titans, Vol. III: Founding Fathers, Women Warriors & WWII
Samuel Adams, Thomas Paine, George Washington, John Adams, Thomas Jefferson, James Madison, Alexander Hamilton, Ben Franklin, Sybil Ludington, James Armistead Lafayette, Elizabeth Cady Stanton, Susan B. Anthony, Harriet Tubman, Adolf Hitler, FDR & Churchill

Liszt's *Dante Symphony*

A historical mystery/thriller highlighting the belligerent rise of Nazi Germany from its Prussian roots, replete with ciphers, spies, murder and a stellar cast, including Albert Einstein, Rossini, Liszt, Nazi officers and Adolf Hitler.

Hardcover: 9780981762548
Paperback: 9780981762531
eBook: 9780997680713

The Winds of Time

The Winds of Time is a historical tour de force of Western civilization by Rich DiSilvio.

With masterful style, DiSilvio paints a fascinating historical canvas with the flare of a consummate artist. Key figures and the primary cultures that literally shaped the Western world are candidly analyzed, revealing both the dark and luminous sides of mankind. Moreover, DiSilvio's insightful essays add intriguing new dimensions to the historical record.

Hardcover: 9780981762524
eBook: 9780997680706

FIRST PLACE WINNER

Meet My Famous Friends

Inspiring kids with Humor!
A whimsical picture book that pays homage to great historical figures in imaginative ways.

Author/Illustrator Rich DiSilvio presents a broad array of geniuses and heroes in a humorous and compelling fashion by altering their names and appearances, whereby making us see very familiar people in very different ways.

While children will get a kick out of looking at the comical artwork, teens and even adults will appreciate the witty play on words, inventive creations, and perhaps glean a thing or two about some of these iconic people who had a great influence on society in one form or another. Their lives and contributions have uplifted humanity in various ways, thus being great role models for young and old alike.

Hardcover: 9780997680751 Paperback: 9780997680768 eBook: 9780997680775

PURPLE DRAGONFLY WINNER

Danny and the DreamWeaver

A MS novelette by Mark Poe (aka Rich DiSilvio) about the power of dreams and the imagination.

When Danny meets Nostrildamus in his dream a bizarre journey begins!

Packed with dry humor, a mystery, and zany-looking artists, like Michelanjello & Hippopotamus Bosch, *Danny and the DreamWeaver* is an imaginative adventure of criminal intrigue and art history that demonstrates the importance of looking at life differently.

Paperback: 9780997680737
eBook: 9780997680744

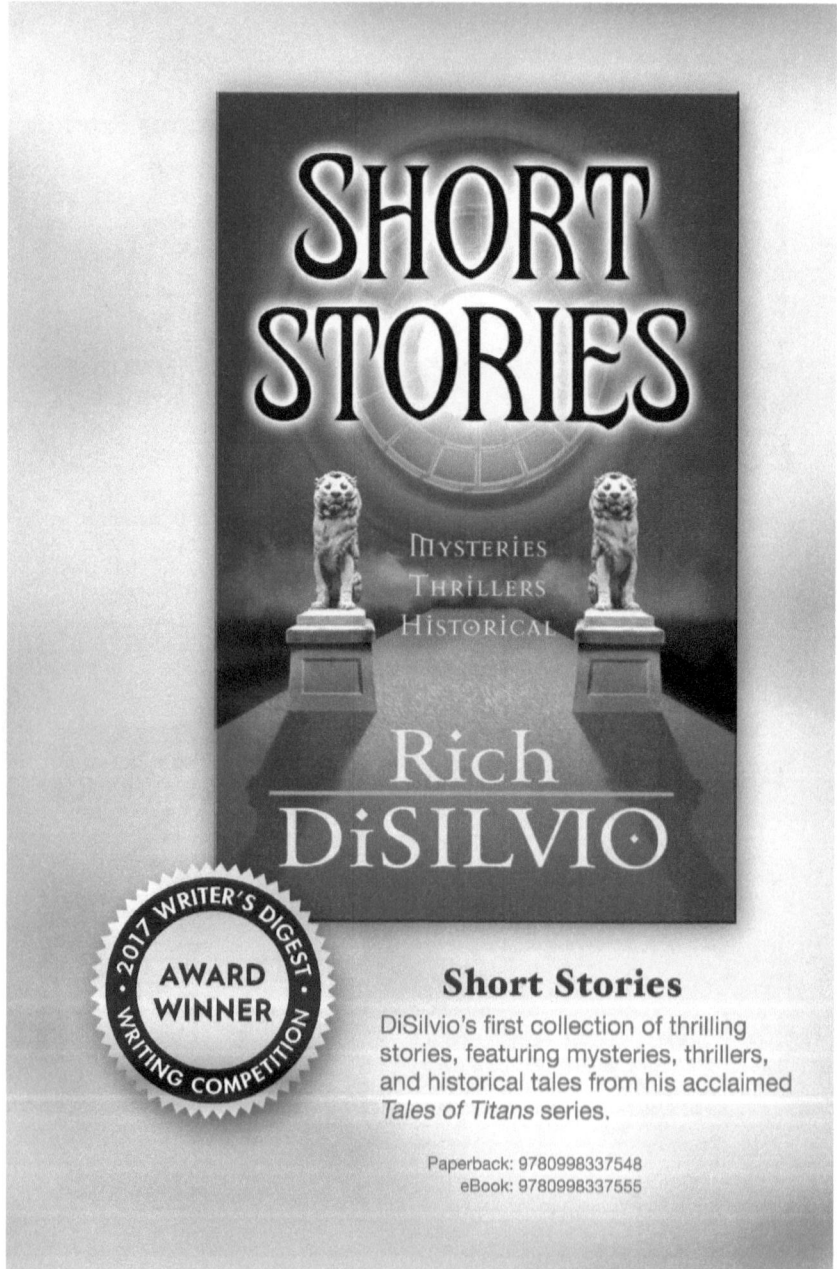

Short Stories

DiSilvio's first collection of thrilling stories, featuring mysteries, thrillers, and historical tales from his acclaimed *Tales of Titans* series.

Paperback: 9780998337548
eBook: 9780998337555

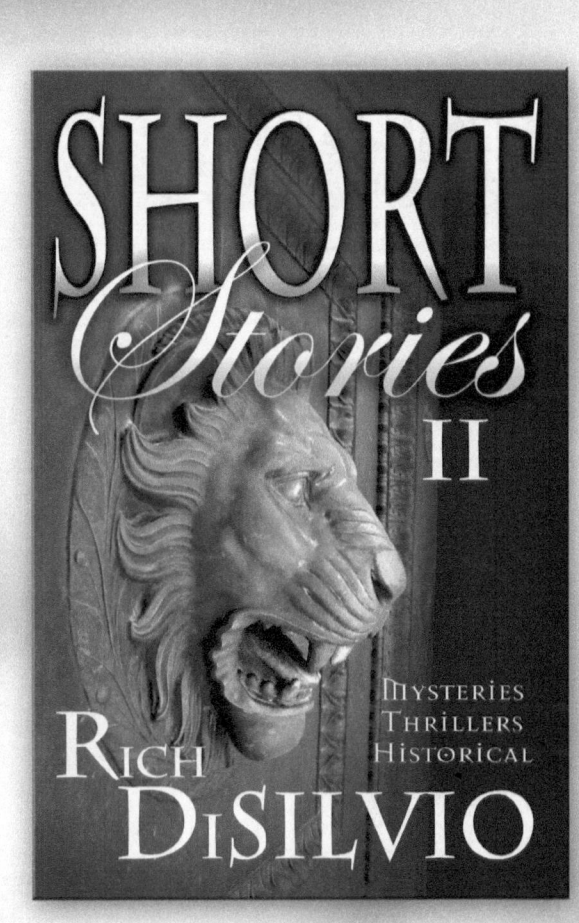

Short Stories II

DiSilvio's second collection of thrilling
stories, featuring mysteries, thrillers,
and historical tales from his acclaimed
Tales of Titans series.

Paperback: 9780998337562
eBook: 9780998337579

Short Stories III

From the vivid imagination of multi-award-winning author/artist Rich DiSilvio comes this spellbinding collection of fantasy and Sci-Fi tales.

Paperback: 9780998337586
eBook: 9780998337593